THE BUFFALO SOLDIER

When Lazarus Brown, sergeant in the Ninth United States Cavalry, a negro outfit, deserted and fled to Mexico after shooting two Lazy Y cowhands for lynching his scout, Indian Charlie, Jason Slade, boss of the Lazy Y, made it a big hunt. A backshooter, Pinkerton agents, even a bandit chief were hired by Slade to get that 'uppity niggra' back across the Rio Grande so that he could have the pleasure of seeing him swing under the hanging tree.

THE BUFFALO SOLDIER

THE BUFFALO SOLDIER

by
Elliot Conway

MAGNA PRINT BOOKS
Long Preston, North Yorkshire,
England.

British Library Cataloguing in Publication Data.

Conway, Elliot
  The buffalo soldier.

ISBN 1-85057-998-9

First Published in Great Britain by Robert Hale Ltd 1988.

Printed and bound in Great Britain by
Redwood Press Limited, Melksham, Wiltshire.

For Doreen Marguerite

One

The horse soldiers rode stoop-backed, easing saddle-tortured limbs. The squeaking of leather and the soft padding of hooves in the ankle-deep, throat-burning dust were the only sounds breaking the monotonous silence that hung over the column.

F Troop detail of Company D, Ninth United States Cavalry, were six days out from Fort Dodds, Texas; somewhere west of the Brazos, chasing Quanah Parker and his Kwahadi Comanche war band's trail-dust.

Troop Sergeant Lazarus Brown rode point with Indian Charlie, the company's 'breed scout. Every bone in his six feet plus frame ached and iron weights pressed down on his eyelids. He could even see lines of fatigue on the usually wooden-faced part-Crow scout.

Captain Terence S Walsh, F Troop commander, eager to come to grips with the enemy, forced his men along at a soul-destroying pace. For too long the Ninth Calvary had seen only the results of the marauding Comanche and Apache. The smouldering ruins of a life's

11

work, the violated, butchered women. The overdue trapper scalped and left spread-eagled on the plains, pinned in a grotesque pattern of death by war lances.

Indian Charlie grunted and pointed to the ground, then his eyes lifted and standing in his stirrups he gave the nearby hills a long searching look. Lazarus saw the horse droppings and the tiredness fell away from him. Horse droppings meant horses and this far out on the plains, miles away from the nearest cattle range, horses meant Comanche. Indian Charlie slipped from his saddle and picked up a ball and rolled it again his cheek. The black button eyes winked bright.

'Fresh, Lazarus,' he said. 'Two hour, m'be three...no more.'

'That near, Charlie?' replied Lazarus. 'They must be holed up in those hills.'

The scout did not answer but set off in a wide nose-to-ground arc like a hound dog strong on the scent of a tree'd 'possum. Lazarus waited patiently, his carbine out of its boot and resting across his saddle-horn, his eyes moving left and right across his horizon until Charlie finished his reading of the trail. If there was anything to be read in the dust Charlie would pick it out. He'd never known him wrong yet, or fooled. Charlie came back to his horse breathing heavily.

'Many pony tracks, Lazarus,' Charlie pant-ed. He held both hands up. 'But only ten with riders on.' He stood silently for a while, face screwed up in concentration. 'M'be Comanche not know that pony soldiers are on their trail. M'be stay night at Sweet Water to water horses.'

Lazarus rubbed at his chin reflectively. 'Could be, Charlie, could be... There's not much water in the hills. If they've got a good remuda of stolen horses they'll not want to run them into the ground. You'll be right about them not thinking that the long-knives are so close to them. The way the Captain's been driv-ing us it's a wonder that the troop is not ahead of them...here he comes now, Charlie. We'll see what he has to say, it's his command.'

Captain Walsh was a man with a big-sized chip riding on his shoulder. The Ninth United States Cavalry, Indian-fighting on the Texas plains, was short of officers. The Ninth's enlisted men, like its sister regiment the Tenth, were all negroes. Rotting in some frontier post commanding a bunch of blacks and fighting an enemy that did not observe the niceties and chivalry of a way of war that had been taught back east did not appeal to Captain Walsh's military ardour. Dusty, fly-pestered Fort

13

Dodds was a long way from the regimental balls and the pretty girls of a more civilized military post. Despite his protests Lt Walsh was posted to the Ninth. To soften the blow he was given another bar and now ranked Captain, commander of Troop F.

He soon realized that the Ninth was a veteran outfit. The 'Buffalo Soldiers', as the Texans called them, skins might be black but they gave as good as any white horse soldier and got more than their fair share of combat duty. This was the new captain's first patrol, and swallowing his prejudices, he fervently blessed the major for including Top Sergeant Lazarus Brown in the detail. Without the big negro's combat experience and the half-breed Crow Indian's trail-reading capabilities he'd have probably led his first command slap into a hostile ambush before the sound of the main gate at Fort Dodds slamming shut behind him had died away. How anyone could find their way in this godforsaken land had him beat. Quanah Parker's bucks could be hidden behind every rock ready to leap out and massacre his entire command. And what he had seen at close quarters of their handiwork still made him shudder. Coming up over the rise Captain Walsh saw his sergeant and the Crow scout conferring together along the rim. He held up a once-white gloved hand and the column shuffled to a halt. He called over his shoulder.

'Troop... Dismount! Flankers out...ease girths! Bugler! Follow me!'

He cantered across to his sergeant. Lazarus touched the drooped brim of his campaign hat. Capt. Walsh held back an angry reprimand about slovenly saluting. It wouldn't do to pull rank. Not just yet. He hadn't been accepted by the men. They'd be watching how he shaped up when the lead began to fly, and he'd been long enough in uniform to know that a good top sergeant, uppity nigger or otherwise, can make or break a rookie captain.

'Charlie thinks that they are not more than two or three hours ahead, sir,' Lazarus said. 'They're driving a herd of stolen horses...that's slowing them down. There's water... Sweet Water...before the trail cuts through the hills. Charlie thinks that there's a good chance they'll stop the night at the water. They could be part of Quanah Parker's war band...the chief could be with them.'

Quanah Parker! Captain Walsh's blood began to surge. If he could pull him in that would shake them up in the mess at Fort Dodds. M'be win him a transfer back east or at least his oak leaves.

'How do we play it?' he said.

Indian Charlie swung his right hand round. 'We go this way, along the edge of the hills and get between the Comanche and the pass.'

Lazarus saw the look of indecision on the captain's face.

'Begging the Captain's pardon but what Charlie says makes sense. The hostiles are bound to have a lookout watching their back trail but if we can sneak up ahead of them... jump them at first light...well, we could be calling the tune.'

Charlie nodded his head in agreement and the parade-ground charge with sabres bared and guidons flapping faded from the Captain's vision. In the short time he had been on the Texas plains he had heard enough about the cunning of the Comanche to savvy what Charlie and the sergeant said made sense. It took a lobo's trick to catch a lobo.

Captain Walsh straightened up in his saddle. 'Right, Sergeant, get the Troop mounted and you, Charlie, get us on to hard ground. I want no giveaway dust-trail to alert the Comanche before the light goes.' The Captain's voice hardened. 'I want them still lying on their blankets when we hit them.'

Two

Indian Charlie dropped to his knees and held up a warning hand. Behind him the troopers, extended in a thin skirmishing line, melted into the ground.

'What is it, Charlie?' whispered an anxious Captain Walsh.

The scout beckoned for him to come forward. The Captain crept up to him and raising himself slightly he peered over the Crow's shoulder and through the pale streaks of mist that hung over the water-hole of Sweet Water. He drew his next breath in with a loud hiss. The basin was dotted with small smokeless fires. Captain Walsh swallowed hard.

Fiercely he snapped, 'I thought that we were only trailing ten braves? The place is swarming with hostiles. The whole damn Comanche nation is here.'

Lazarus, who had joined them, said, 'There were only ten, Captain. The water-hole must be the meeting place for several war bands. I've counted at least thirty bucks.'

All Captain Walsh's uncertainties returned.

He knew that it was make or break time. Then he thought of all the decisions younger officers than him had had to make during the Civil War. Momentous decisions affecting the outcome of great battles, not some penny-ante plains skirmish that would not make two lines in the papers back east. He took another look at the Comanche encampment, this time a look of appraisal. This side of the fires he could see the pony lines. Beyond the camp, in a narrow draw, he saw the rearing heads and swishing tails of at least forty horses. The hostiles' bank account. He lowered himself and spoke to his two men. His orders were curt and precise. West Point would have been proud of him.

'Sergeant, you take eight men and get between the camp and the horses. There's a dry wash running across the front of the pony lines where you can get your men under cover. You will then commence firing. That will draw the Comanche to the horses. To get to them they will have to cross a stretch of open ground. I intend to make it the killing ground by putting the rest of the men out on the left flank. With a bit of luck we ought to break them in our crossfire.'

Lazarus looked at the Captain with a bit more respect. He was learning. If Captain Walsh lived long enough he would make a good Indian-fighter.

'It could work at that, sir,' he said. 'I'd better take Charlie. They're bound to have a watch at the pony lines.'

'Fine,' replied Captain Walsh. 'Just give me enough time to get my men into position before you start firing...good luck, Sergeant.'

Lazarus and Indian Charlie crawled, dirt-bellied, along the line of ponies. The sergeant touched the scout on the back and put his mouth to his ear.

'Over there! In front of that pinto...see him?'

The scout looked under the steaming bellies and saw the legs of the horse guard. Lazarus saw the glint of steel in his mouth as the scout sidled away from him. He heard the Comanche clear his throat but before he could spit he saw the bare legs jerk several times, then the Comanche's whole body came into view as Indian Charlie lowered it to the ground. Lazarus waved his men forward.

He positioned his section along the rim of the wash and slowly counted to a hundred. That was all the time he could allow the captain. Daylight was coming up fast and once the Comanche got to their feet the troop had lost what little advantage they had. He brought up

19

his carbine in line with the nearest sleeping buck and squeezed the trigger. The 40.40 ball hammered the Indian into the ground. Its roar was echoed by the rest of the detail's fire.

The fusillade exploded the encampment into life. Near-naked bucks jumped up from their blankets, some falling back as the deadly hail took its toll. The rest, in one blood-curdling, screaming flood of hate, came at Lazarus and his men. The sergeant feverishly began to count off the seconds he had left to live. Eight rifles could not stop the kill-crazy warriors. They would tear them to pieces with their bare hands. A line of red flames flared away to his left. Then another, and another. And Lazarus began to think that he would see a new dawn through.

The charging Indians, caught on their flank by the rapid volley fire, milled around in panicky disorder. Four times the flanking rifles fired in unison, their terrible barrage cutting the Comanche down like a giant scythe.

A bugle sounded shrill and clear above the yelling and the shooting, and Captain Walsh's men spilled out into the open, their guns still exacting their deadly toll.

'Let's go!' yelled Lazarus and followed by his detail scrambled out of the wash, reloading, firing as they walked. Everything to Lazarus became a blur of smoke and flame. He saw two of his men drop to the ground arrow shot. The two lines of Buffalo soldiers converged and began herding the Comanche into a tight half-circle away from their only chance of escape, their ponies. The eagle-feathered chief made one last desperate attempt to break the horse soldiers' ring. He came at the troopers at a run, hatchet held high. His death hulloes were cut short as a full volley from Captain Walsh's line ripped his chest into a bloody mess. Then it was all over.

An examination of the Comanche dead and prisoners took a little of the edge off Captain Walsh's first combat victory. Quanah Parker was not in either tally.

Three

Indian Charlie, riding up ahead, saw the riders first, or leastways he saw their trail-dust. A long heavy cloud that meant a lot of riders. He rode back to the column but Lazarus had already seen what had alarmed the scout. The detail had split up. Lazarus and eight troopers were escorting the prisoners taken at Sweet Water back to the reservation, Captain Walsh and the rest of the men herding the stolen horses back to Fort Dodds where their former owners could collect them.

Lazarus waited anxiously for the riders to show themselves. If it was another band of hostiles it was a big one. Too big for nine men to fight off and watch out for the prisoners.

The riders came nearer and Lazarus saw that they were Texans. By the way they were armed they meant business and it was not Church Meeting Day business. The Texans halted alongside the troop and the troopers, aware of the tetchiness of many Texans towards the Buffalo soldiers, sensed possible white man/ black boy trouble and closed up on their sergeant.

Lazarus assessed the thickset, heavy-jowled man in the well cut broadcloth. He had all the makings of the bossman. Lazarus noted the brand marks of the Lazy Y on the flanks of the big man's wild-eyed roan. A hard horse for a hard man, he thought. The fleshy man spoke. It was a rasping, used-to-being obeyed, voice. The voice of a man who would take no sass from an uppity nigger in or out of uniform.

'We'll take those red nigras off yuh, boy.'

Lazarus's back stiffened in anger at the use of the word boy for a grown black man. He thought of all the 'boys' of the Ninth and Tenth

Calvary lying, army-issue-blanket-wrapped in their shallow graves out there on the plains so that high and mighty Texicans could raise their herds in peace. Lazarus hard-eyed him.

'These Comanche are going back to the reservation, Mister...whoever you are. Captain's orders.'

The big rancher flinched as though Lazarus had struck him a blow and his fleshy face quivered in hardly-controlled rage.

'I'm Jason Slade, boss of this outfit. Now ah'll tell yuh once more, boy, just in case yuh're hard of hearing...hand over those murdering varmints. Hostiles burnt out two of mah line cabins last night...killed three of mah men...run off with some beef. So ah aim to string up any hostile ah can get mah hands on. Now just be sensible, boy, then we can all go on our ways.'

Out of the corner of his eye Lazarus saw Slade's crew stir restlessly in their saddles, hands edging to their guns. He knee'd his horse alongside Slade's and brought the hand hidden from the rancher across his horse's neck and rammed the long-barrelled cavalry pistol into his belly. Slade's grunt of pain lowered Lazarus's temperature a little.

'Haul off, Mister Slade.' The sergeant's voice was iron-hard. 'The plantation days are over,

23

so don't try anything. This pistol is loaded in all chambers. I'll get you for sure, m'be a couple of your men before I go down. If you like those odds make your play. If not, back off. In any case we're coming through.' Lazarus grinned. 'Marster.'

The nervous shuffling of horses' hooves was the only sound to break the silence as soldiers and ranch-hands watched each other like a pack of wild dogs stiff-legged in anticipation of a fight. Indian Charlie moved up to the far side of Slade, crowding him, the scout's rifle out of its loop, muzzle pointed inwards. Slade's eyes narrowed to needle points of hate. The words came out as though begrudged.

'It looks like a Mexican stand-off, black boy. But we'll meet again. Yuh can bank on that.' Savagely he pulled the roan's head around, ignoring Lazarus's pistol. Over his shoulder he called out, 'And that goes double fur yuh, 'breed.' Then raising his voice he shouted: 'All right, boys, let's ride. We'll finish this business another day.'

Lazarus and Indian Charlie watched them ride away, their dust blowing back into their faces. Lazarus holstered his pistol and ran a hand across his brow.

'Charlie,' he croaked. 'I'd rather face a Comanche war band any day.'

'You look out for yourself, Lazarus,' Indian Charlie said. 'I know this man Slade. He's big in the territory, big and mean. You made him eat crow an' that goes agin' his righteous hatred of Indians and nigras.'

It was a big speech for Indian Charlie but Lazarus agreed with every word of it.

Four

The three Lazy Y cow-hands rode slowly along letting the cool morning air clear liquor-fuddled brains, but the fresh breeze did nothing to clear Wichita's mind of his lost pay. He was a small weasel of a man and a bad loser. He was thinking how hard it had been to earn his two dollars a day and all found. The dust and stink of the cattle drive, fighting off bad Indians way up beyond the Canadian. Staying away from the bad women and bad liquor of Abilene. Then only to lose it all on Big Rosie's crooked gambling tables before he had time to pay a call on that new yella-skinned girl Rosie had brung in from across the Rio Grande.

A cow-hand's life was worse than a mangy cur dog's. He had a burning itch to down someone as low as he felt. Providing the odds were in his favour. His mournful thoughts were broken by Lafe's voice.

'Hey, Mex!' he heard him say. 'Ain't that the shack of the soldier boys' 'breed scout? The one Ketch told us about. Him and that buck nigra sergeant...how the old man nearly bust a gut when the pair of them made him back down...remember?'

A mean smile came into Wichita's face. 'Why don't we ride on down thar' and make him dance a jig justa knock some of the sass outa him? Thar's some right fine trees hereabouts.'

Lafe let out a whoop. 'Just like we did tuh that stinkin' skinner. Come on, Mex, let's see if the squaw man's at home.'

Indian Charlie sat on the edge of his cot holding his head in his hands. He had the almightiest of hangovers. He couldn't remember how long he had been hitting the bottle...two..three days m'be. But he knew that it was taking longer to drown out the nightmares. He must have more of the Crow blood in him than he thought. T'ain't nice killing at the best of times but killing your own kind for people that don't give a damn about you...well. Why couldn't he have been a full-blood, then he would have known where his loyalties lay? Maudlin tears began to flow as he rocked to and fro mumbling the Crow war chant.

The sudden bursting in of the shack's door brought him quickly to his feet and diving across the floor for his knife; but he was too late. After a brief struggle a kick on the side of his head by one of his assailants blacked Charlie out.

When he came round Charlie found himself standing under a tree, hands tied behind his back, and a noose laid slackly around his neck. He began to sober up fast. There were three of them and he took them to be Lazy Y men. The small pinched-faced man standing in front of him shouted,

'Up he goes, boys!'

The rope jerked and Charlie felt the noose tighten as he was pulled up onto his toes. The veins in his neck began to swell as he gasped and grunted for breath.

The small man laughed. 'Dance, yuh red bastard, dance.' He kicked Charlie's feet from under him making the rope take all his weight. The scout's eyeballs bulged and his tongue hung out as the rope slowly and painfully choked the life out of him. His wildly scrambling feet found the ground again, easing the terrible pressure of the rope, allowing him to gulp in a few breaths of life-saving air. Grinning, the Lazy Y man made to kick at his feet again. This time Charlie was ready. He kicked out with one foot catching his tormentor low down. The man cursed and doubled up in pain.

'The bastard's crippled me,' the man cried out.

Behind him Charlie heard the two on the rope laugh and though balancing precariously on his toes, gasping for breath, he managed a smile himself. There was no humour in the small man's face when he hobbled past Charlie. Viciously he snarled,

'Ah'll swing yuh for keeps, red man.'

The rope was pulled sharply and Charlie's body arched and thrashed like a hooked fish as the life was choked out of him.

The Mex, white-faced sober, looked with wide-eyed horror at the slowly rotating body. 'Sweet Jesus,' he cried. 'Ah'm getting to hell outa here—ah didn't expect to be a party to a lynching!'

Lafe was too busy throwing up to answer him. Wichita remained silent, his faro losses forgotten. The Mex was right. The sooner they put some distance between them and what they had done the better. He'd definitely known better days than this.

Before they reached Lazy Y land the trio met Ketch, the ranch's straw-boss. Lafe, mind still on the swinging body, babbled out what had happened. Ketch gave them a withering look.

'Yuh all had a right good end of trail bust-up, didn't yuh. Did anyone see yuh?'

'Ah don't reckon so,' said the Mex. 'We got outa there damn fast...left him still decorating the tree.'

Ketch sucked at his teeth. 'The boss will have to be told. Could be serious, army business. The 'breed was on their payroll and the Yankee blue-bellies won't take kindly tuh no-good Texicans who can't hold their liquor stringing up one of their scouts.' Ketch reflected for a while then: 'Yuh best get over to the line cabin at Grassy Canyon and lie low there for a day or two 'til it blows over. If yuh have been seen we don't want yuh picked out as Lazy Y men.'

Ketch watched them ride away, cursing under his breath. His hair had gone grey wet-nursing cattle; he wasn't about to lose it wet-nursing cow-hands. He would let Slade sort it out.

'As ah've said, Mr Slade,' Ketch finished. 'It was a bit of horseplay that went wrong.'

Slade had listened in silence as his foreman had told him the score. He wasn't opposed to neck-stretching. Why there had been a time, when he had just started building the herd and

29

before the local cattle-lifters and owl-hoots got the measure of him, he had almost run out of trees to hang them all on. But it had been done legal-like, within the law, and in this part of Texas, before the blasted blue-bellied horse soldiers moved in, that meant his law. Out-and-out lynching got hanging a bad name.

'Yuh did right, Ketch,' he agreed. 'What's done is done. Keep them outa sight for a while. If those Yankees at the Fort find out that the Lazy Y had a hand in the killing they could cancel mah beef contract.'

Five

For the next few days Lazarus was too busy with the routine duties of the Fort, training new recruits to take the place of those killed at Sweet Water, to worry too much about Slade's threat. He saw Captain Walsh heading in his direction so he dismissed the troopers and waited for the captain to come up to him.

Captain Walsh returned his salute, then said, 'We're moving out in four day's time, Sergeant. Three companies...it's a big operation. The Tenth are coming down from Fort Worth.

Between us we should be able to nail Quanah Parker before he can slip over the Rio Grande. If you and Indian Charlie come to my quarters after duty we can go over our part in the campaign. By the way, have you seen the scout lately?'

Lazarus smiled. 'He'll turn up before long, sir. He generally has a two- or three-day drinking session when he gets back from a patrol. It kinda upsets him killing his own kind, him being best-part Indian. But if he doesn't show up by chow-time I'll ride over and roust him out.'

Indian Charlie had not made an appearance by mess-call and Lazarus began to worry. The lamps had been lit at the Fort by the time the sergeant reached the scout's ramshackle hut. The hut was in darkness and Charlie's horse snickered a welcome from a small stand of timber but there was no sign of Charlie. Lazarus came over cold. Something smelt wrong. He dismounted and walking over to the hut pushed open the unlocked door. He struck a match and saw the upturned table and the broken chair and his fears became justified. He cursed as the match burned his fingers. Lazarus picked up the storm lantern, lit it and looked round the cabin. The embers in the hearth were cold and lowering the lantern for a closer

31

look he noticed the twin drag-marks of boot heels zigzagging across the dirt floor. He followed them out. The scuff marks ended where three shod horses had stood. Lazarus's face set like carved ebony.

He did not have to cut any more sign. He knew where Charlie would be. Lazarus walked into the stand of cottonwoods, fearful and apprehensive. Ten feet in, Charlie's feet bumped into his face. He held the lantern high and reached up and felt the scout's legs. They were as stiff as boards, he had been there at least a day. Slade's men had not taken long to extract payment for their boss's injured pride. Savagely he threw the lantern away.

He loosened the rope and let Charlie down and with the body resting uneasily over his shoulder he made his way back to the cabin. Lazarus laid Charlie's body on the table and prepared it for its last camp. He washed it and dressed it in a clean shirt. From one of the cabin walls he took down a heavily patterned blanket, Charlie's only remembrance of his full-blooded Crow mother, and wrapped it round the scout.

Lazarus went outside and below the trees he dug the grave. When it was deep enough he returned to the cabin and stood silent for a minute or two over Indian Charlie. He would have liked to spend a night's vigil over the body but he had to get back to the Fort. Charlie would understand. He also had a lot of thinking to do. After he had filled in the grave Lazarus piled stones on top to keep out the carrion-eaters and on the wooden marker he scratched the words...'Here lies Indian Charlie, U.S Army scout. Killed by no-good whites.'...

He saw to it that Charlie's horse had food and water for the night and tethered it on a long rope so that it could not wander away. He would have need for it tomorrow. After a last look at Charlie's grave he rode back to the Fort. Slowly and thoughtfully.

He had been a young shave-tail recruit when he first met Indian Charlie. Now the Civil War was over the negro was reaching for a place in the sun but the whites were not yet ready to accept the black man as an equal. Even the whorehouses barred black soldiers. Black regiments were posted to the arid plains of Texas campaigning against the Comanche and the Apache. The only whites were the settlers and the ranchers who had no use for the Yankees, carpet-bagger or soldier, white or black, especially black blue-bellies.

Indian Charlie had taken a liking to him, taught him the way it was on the plains. Lazarus had told him of his raising on a Minnesota dirt farm. How he had been accused of being an Uncle Tom by some of his kin for joining a white man's army. Indian Charlie had known all about that, him being a half-breed, an outcast from his own tribe for working for the pony soldiers in hunting down his own kind. Lazarus soon recognized a kindred spirit in Indian Charlie, an inbetween, not all white yet working for them, killing for them. As he had done since.

The scout had been like an elder brother to him. Taught him how to bend with the wind on both sides of the race divide so that he could survive in a white man's world. He had been a quick learner and began to work his way up through the ranks. Now he was more soldier than black man. But Indian Charlie lying in his lonely grave had turned the clock back. He was a negro once more and proud of it. He had proved himself as good as any white soldier. He had also taken a white man's orders and biddings for the last time. All the decisions he would make from here on in would be his... right or wrong.

Six

Next day Lazarus was up before the sun had lifted above the rim of the plain. He was dressed in his civilian levis and with his warbag under his arm he silently left his room. His only link with the U.S Cavalry was his Dragoon Colt pistol, his campaign hat and a ramrod back. He climbed over the Fort palisade by way of the low roof of the stables while the sentries at the main gate stood huddled around the guard fire on the parapet. Once out of sight of the Fort he broke into a run.

Back in Charlie's cabin Lazarus took down the scout's battered stock Winchester from its pegs. It was an old gun but accurate, as Lazarus had seen on many a patrol. Searching round he found a box of reloads for the long gun and also Charlie's Bowie, honed to a fine killing edge. He saddled up Charlie's horse and slipped the Winchester into its loop. In the saddlebags were all the dry rations, for horse and rider, he had collected in the cabin. He was as ready as he would ever be for what might lie ahead.

He took another look at the tracks outside the cabin. As he had seen by lantern-light one of the horses had a left back shoe loose. It was a lead, a thin one, to the killers of Charlie. Lazarus mounted Charlie's horse and heeled it into a steady trot. He had turned his back on Fort Dodds. It was as though his army life had never existed.

The sun was well across the sky before Lazarus had the feeling that he was nearing the end of his trail. He rode along, all senses alert. This was Lazy Y land, Slade's kingdom. He could be riding into a necktie party. He came to a place where another rider had joined the three he was tracking. He got off his horse to examine the sign more closely. The horse with the loose shoe and two others broke away from the main trail and headed across open range.

The line cabin squatted lopsidedly at the mouth of a narrow draw. Standing in a small corral were three horses. Lazarus came down to the shack on foot, shirt-carrying the Dragoon. He had his marksman's badge but he was no fast-draw man. His only advantage was that a man only had to be hit once with the heavy slug the Dragoon threw. That meant three shots. The men in the cabin, seeing him without a rifle or a belted handgun, might just give him that much time.

Nearing the cabin Lazarus saw two men sitting on its broken-planked porch. After a quick look about he placed the third man inside the shack. He walked, stiff-legged, as tensed up as a town dog in heat, past the men, keeping them on his left on his way to the corral. Before he could check the horses for the tell-tale loose shoe one of the men on the porch said,

'Keep away from those horses, nigra, or I'll ventilate yuhr black hide.'

Lazarus ignored the warning and kept on going. The cold hardness pressing against his belly gave him some comfort but the sweat of fear was beaded on his brow. The cow-hand who had spoken called over his shoulder.

'Hey, Lafe, better come on out, thar's another neck wants stretching.'

Lazarus had no doubts now that he was on the right trail. Before there were three guns on the porch he made his play. Swinging round on the balls of his feet he dropped down on one knee and tugged at the Dragoon, its foresight tearing at his chest as it cleared his shirt. The pistol boomed twice in the narrow confines of the draw. The man who had spoken about the neck-stretching pitched over onto his face, his gun still sheathed at his hip. His pardner, halfway to his feet, caught Lazarus's second shot full in the chest, flinging him backwards, back against the man with the rifle who had come running out of the hut. Before the rifleman could regain his balance Lazarus laid the pistol across his left forearm and snapped off another shot. The man let out a banshee yell and fell to the floor. For a while Lazarus heard the wild drumming of his heels on the dry boards. Then silence once more came over the canyon.

Lazarus straightened up. It was an unsteady hand that held the gun. He had never killed in cold blood before. Never killed a white man before. Slade would need no Western Union telegraph to tell him who was responsible for the shootings. He had signed his own death warrant. He had to get out of Texas before someone was sent to serve the warrant. Although his army career was finished and every white man in Texas would join in the hunt for him, he would do it all again. A man shouldn't have to stand being stomped on all his life. He should be able to walk tall now and again. Charlie never got that chance. The Slades of this world saw to that. Now Indian Charlie had been avenged and Slade's bigotted mind would never understand why. To him Indians and Negroes didn't have feelings of loyalty. Didn't have normal white folk feelings like lovin' and sadness. Sometime in the future, if he could stay alive, Jason Slade would get to know just how deep those feelings ran.

Lazarus went back to his horse. He reloaded the pistol, sheathed it, then belted it about his middle. He mounted and took a quick look at the surrounding country. He could see no ominous dust-trails. He pulled the horse's head round and rode off the Lazy Y range to the comparative safety of the open plain.

Seven

Slade, busy working on his tally ledgers, looked up with annoyance when the door of his den flew open. Without looking up from his books he barked:

'Don't yuh bother tuh knock nowadays?'

'They're all dead, boss!' blurted out Ketch.

Slade looked at the strain-faced Ketch. 'Who the hell's all dead?' he demanded.

'Lafe, the Mex, Wichita. The whole three of them. Ah found them lying there at the line cabin...gun shot.'

Slade got quickly to his feet knocking the ledgers off the desk in his haste.

'Comanche,' he said more or less to himself.

39

'But we've had no news of any war band being out.'

His foreman shook his head. 'Weren't Comanche, boss. No scalping, nothing like that. Ah found three shell-cases. Big pistol empties. M'be as heavy as the blue-belly horse soldiers favour.'

Slade's lips curled back from his teeth in a fierce grimace. 'That big black sonuvabitch. Ah'll see him hang. It could only have been him. The 'breed backed him up that day when they brought those hostiles in.'

'It mightn't be that easy, boss. On the way over ah heard talk from the Fort sutler that a top sergeant has deserted. He also said that the army found the scout nice and neat like, marker 'an all.'

'That proves it then, Ketch. He musta buried the 'breed before going on tuh the line cabin. Get as many of the crew yuh can spare and pick up his tracks from the line cabin. Have a couple of the hands swing north, up as far as the Red. Just in case he's high-tailed it that way. But ah've got a gut feeling that he's heading south for Mexico. Manuel!' Slade yelled. When the Mexican steward appeared in the doorway he said, 'Mah horse out front, pronto. Ah've some telegraphs tuh send. Then get the buckboard out and ride over tuh

Grassy Canyon. There's three ex Lazy Y cow-hands lying there.' Then turning back to Ketch. 'Get him before the army picks him up. Ah don't want him jailed. Ah want the murderer tuh hang.'

Ketch, a fair man, said, 'It weren't murder, Mr Slade. All three were kilt face-on...' Slade glared at him. Ketch swallowed hard. 'Ah'll get the men mounted straightaway, boss.'

Eight

Lazarus kept to the back trails on his ride to the border. It would take him a day longer to reach the Rio Grande but it would be safer. He reckoned that Slade would have only had time to cover the main routes to Mexico. Another thing he was gambling on was that the rancher couldn't be certain that his quarry was heading south. That indecision could mean the difference between life or death for Lazarus.

Lazarus came down from the hills; ahead the trail twisted around a steep-sided, cleft-riddled butte. At some time the rock face had split causing a rocky tumble to partially block

41

the track. Beyond the rocks it was open un-
dulating country with scarce enough cover to
hide a jack-rabbit. A watcher stationed on the
butte rim could see a horseman miles away
across the flat.

Suddenly Lazarus's horse gave a coughing
grunt and fell forward onto its knees. Then
he heard the sound of the shot booming back
from the rock face. Lazarus kicked his feet
out of the stirrups and yanked his rifle out
of its sling as he flung himself dirtwards,
rolling behind the shelter of a boulder as he
hit the ground. The second shot raised the
dust at his heels. Looking behind him he saw
his horse, blood gushing from its mouth, keel
over onto its side. Its back legs jerked spas-
modically then with a deep groaning sigh it lay
still.

Lazarus cursed. He had to give that bastard
Slade his due. He could move fast. But that
did not give him any excuse for allowing
himself to be bushwhacked. Not after all Indian Charlie had taught him. Lazarus sneaked
a quick look over his shelter, drawing a third
shot that sent splinters of rock flying into his
face. And also pinpointed the sniper's hide-
away. He was halfway up a narrow crack in the
butte face some hundred and fifty yards away.
Lazarus felt the warm trickle of blood running

down his face from the rock splash. It gave him an idea. He grinned savagely. Got you, you sonuvabitch, he thought.

Flat on his belly, raising as much dust as a moving rattler, Lazarus reached a point almost opposite the sniper's cleft. He paused for a minute or two to get his breathing more regular and to steady his hands, checked that the Winchester was fully loaded then brought it up to his shoulder, fast. In a calico-ripping sound he triggered off the full magazine. He could not see his target but fired at the left side of the cleft. Above the sound of the whining ricochets he heard a man's scream of pain and the sound of something metallic hitting the rocky floor.

Lazarus reloaded the Winchester, watched and waited for any sign or movement of the sniper, then closed in on the cleft from the right. He saw the rifle, butt-splintered and red-stained. Now you know, whoever you are, that rock splinters can be as dangerous as lead, Lazarus said to himself. He still saw no sign of the sniper. Somehow, in spite of his wound, he must have climbed up to the top of the butte and Lazarus knew that he had lost the chance of a horse.

He would have liked to cross the flat at night but that would cost time and time was what

43

he had none of. He returned to his dead mount and unloaded his warbag and the canteen of water and a blanket. The saddle he left. Its weight would hold him back.

Nine

Lazarus had only got a few hundred yards on the open plain when he heard the screeching of a badly-greased wagon wheel. He put his warbag onto the ground and lay down behind it. Flattening himself as low as possible in the slight dip behind it, he laid his rifle across the top of the bundle and placed a handful of shells alongside it. Before they finished him off they would know what type of man the Ninth Cavalry bred.

The wagon that rattled across the flat was a sunbleached, springless plains monstrosity. What remained of its tarp cover flapped like a Company's guidons. Its driver, an old man in a faded dustcoat and droop-brimmed hat, seemed as old as the wagon itself. Lazarus picked up the Winchester and the shells and got to his feet. The smell of the uncured hides hit him in the face like a blow from a fist. He

44

thought that the skinner was asleep on the high seat but the Sharps that the old man cradled across his knee moved slightly in his direction. A pair of eyes that had not lost their brightness looked him over. The old man spat brown.

'Yuh'll be the big nigra the whole territory is lookin' fur. The one with the big bounty on his hide.'

Lazarus brought his rifle up. Another brown stream shot over the mule's rump and the old man growled.

'Ah wouldn't if ah was yuh. Ah could'av picked yuh off a ways back with this here buf-fli' gun if ah wanted tuh.'

Lazarus met his stare. 'If you want to earn that bounty you'd better use that cannon you're holding. No one's stretching my neck.'

The old skinner's jaws stopped their chomping. 'Ther yuh go, all-fired tetchy. Who said anything about wanting tuh take yuh? Ah want no bounty, tho' ah'll admit it's a sizeable one. Ah reckon it's about time that those road agents and dry-gulchers that pass fur cow-hands on the Lazy Y were cut down tuh size. Ah heerd that yuh kilt three of them, sneaky, Injun-like, as they lay peaceable in their beds.'

'You heard wrong, mister,' replied Lazarus. 'They got better odds than they gave my friend. It took three of them to lynch him.'

The old man nodded. 'Ah reckon that'd be the way of it. Slade's cow-hands have never slept peaceable in their beds since they were babes in arms. They lie uneasy all night, tossing and turning, thinking of new ways tuh stomp on poor folk like me. That Slade thinks he's the Lord Almighty the way he roughshods over everybody...See this!' the old man almost yelled at Lazarus, pulling at the collar of his dustcoat.

On the old man's neck Lazarus saw the angry red weal of a recent rope burn.

'This is what the sons-of-bitches that Slade 'as on his payroll did when they found me watering Jubal here at one of their water-holes. They said ah was polluting their water. Their water! By God. After all the work ah've done killin' the vermin that pesters the dogies.'

For several moments the skinner chewed savagely at his plug.

'The no-good Texicans laughed when they strung me up,' he continued. 'They cut me down just before ah was set tuh meet Saint Peter, then booted me outa camp and said that the next time they found me stinking out their water-holes they'd string me up for good.' The old man chewed a bit more. 'Yuh'll never make it tuh the Rio Grande, son,' he said. 'The word's gone out. It's open season on buck nigras. They stretched out all along the river.'

'Mexico's my only chance,' Lazarus told the skinner. 'They'll hunt me down like a mad dog in Texas.'

The old man rasped his thumb nail across his stubbled chin.

'M'be ah can get yuh tuh the border, if yuh don't mind the stink. Tho' ah reckon that if yuh've fought against Quanah Parker a strong smell won't put yuh out none.'

'Anything's better than Slade's rope,' said Lazarus. 'But I don't want you to end up alongside me under the hanging tree.'

The old man grunted. 'That'll be the day when ah let those sons-of-bitches sneak up on me again. Not while ah'm holding this.' He waved the Sharps at Lazarus.

The old man reached out and handed Lazarus a plug of tobacco.

'Here, son. Take a bite of this before yuh climb aboard. It'll stop yuhr belly coming up into yuhr craw. The smell back there ain't exactly as sweet as a El Paso cat-house.'

Lazarus lost all sense of time lying under the coyote skins. His body ached all over with the bouncing of the wagon.

The wagon ground to a halt and Lazarus flung back the hides. He was almost more ready to face Slade's hunters than stomach the fleas and the maggots and the stink.

'Hold it, son.' The old man spoke without turning his head. 'Thur's two riders at the crossing. Come sundown yuh can sneak across without them seeing yuh. Ah'll camp here just so they don't get suspicious.'

An hour after dark the old man told Lazarus it was safe to come down from the wagon. Lazarus thanked him for his help and shook him by the hand. The old man told him to think nothing of it but that he would be right obliged if he, Lazarus, would ventilate a few more Lazy Y hides if he ever got the chance. Lazarus told him that he'd gun down the whole crew rather than end up swinging on the end of a rope. Before he left, the old man gave Lazarus some advice.

'That flea-dog town across the river,' he said, 'is Coahati. Ah'd steer clear of it. There's bully boys in it that would gut-shoot yuh fur yuhr hat-band let alone the bounty yuh're carrying. If yuh keep walking for three, four days yuh oughta reach a Mex village where they ain't heerd of Jason Slade.' The old man ruminated for a while then he said, 'If yuh get that fur and head due west towards the Candelarias, and if yuh can cross the desert on foot, yuh'll reach the Hacienda Torrea-de-Carros. Its owner, Amos Bismark, has no reason to think fondly of Jason Slade. He should be able tuh offer yuh a place tuh give yuh time tuh sort out what yuh intend tuh do with yuhself.'

After a final handshake Lazarus crept silently down to the river. Keeping a wary eye on the campfire at the ford he made a bundle of his clothes and with his pistol-belt and Winchester slung across his shoulders he held the bundle high as he slipped mother-naked into the water. Just as noiseless he waded chest-deep to the far shore.

On the far bank Lazarus, not bothering to dry himself, quickly dressed. Dawn came up fast in the south-west. The further he was from the Rio Grande before daylight the safer he would feel. He did not want to start watching his back trail so soon. Those days would come. From now on in until he was well away from the border it would be night marches and cold camps. By now the man on the butte or the finding of his dead horse would have told them that he had crossed the border. The Rio Grande would be no barrier against Slade's revenge. But Mexico was a big country and he wanted to keep his trackers guessing for as long as he could in what direction he was heading. The fewer people saw him the longer that time would stretch out. M'be fool them into thinking that he had crossed back into Texas.

Within an hour, in spite of the chilly night air blowing from the bottom lands, he began to dry out. Another six miles into Chihuahua State, Lazarus began to get damp again, this time with sweat. The trail ran south by west, tumbling in and out of fierce hostile mesquite and chaparral-covered dry washes, that tore at his flesh and clothes. The moon was full and high and Lazarus reckoned, in spite of the snaking of the trail, he was making good time and what was equally important, still travelling south.

Ten

Jason Slade thought big, lived big, so it wasn't in his nature to keep his anger under a tight rein. His bullroar as he ranted at his foreman on the porch of the big house rattled the window shutters.

'How could yuh not get him? How many black bastards are there out there on the plains, eh? Yuh'd half the crew, every saddle-tramp and get-rich-quick hombre in the south-west searching for him and yuh let the black sonavabitch get across the Rio Grande and out of

United States jurisdiction.' Slade waved an arm in an angry gesture of dismissal. 'Get back tuh tending the herd, that's if yuh ain't lost that.'

The rancher rammed his cigar back into his mouth and turned to the tall narrow-shouldered man leaning against the side of the house, his face still working in anger. As he chewed savagely at his cigar Slade took stock of the well-worn levis, the scuffed, down-at-heel boots, the mean dead-eyed face. West Texas was crawling with suchlike drifters. Not enough grit to be genuine dyed-in-the-wool shootists or owl-hoots. Bushwhacking was more in their line. They'd backshoot their best friend to raise the price of their next visit to the whorehouse.

'So yuh're Macabe,' Slade said. 'The shootist from away across in New Mexico.' Slade's lips drew back in a disbelieving sneer. 'Yuh don't look nothing special tuh me.'

The beanpole of a man suddenly straightened up and the heavy Colt pistol that had been sheathed low down on his right hip came out and up in a blur of movement. The two rapid barks echoed under the porch roof and the tips of the big bull's horns nailed up on the horse corral gate forty feet away splintered into dozens of shining, whirling fragments. With

51

the same fluid movement the gun was slipped back into its sheath.

Macabe smiled a broken-toothed smile. 'Is that fancy enough, Mr Slade?'

Slade almost choked on his cigar. The horns belonged to Caesar, the Aberdeen-Angus bull that had started off his herd. He had fought Utes, Comanche, Apache and plain everyday Mexican cut-throats to hang onto his herd. Over the years the horns had become his talisman, his symbol of success. Now that no-good sonavabitch had destroyed them. Once Macabe had done what he had been sent for Slade promised himself that he would neck-stretch him from the handiest tree. Just a little. But enough for Macabe to reflect that it did not pay to fool around with Jason Slade. Somehow Slade held his anger in check. He glared balefully at the gunman.

'My foreman will have told yuh what yuh've got tuh do,' he growled. 'There's a hundred in gold for yuh, an extra fifty if yuh can get him back whole so he can stand under the hanging tree.'

'Ah ain't shot a nigra before,' replied Macabe. 'It might be worth losing fifty bucks.'

'That's yuhr business, Mister Macabe,' Slade said. 'Yuh just bring him back here alive or wrapped up in a tarp, yuh'll get yuhr due. We reckon that he's across in Mexico. But that should be no problem. There can't be many six foot tall buck nigras prowling about in the State of Chihuahua.'

Slade watched Macabe ride away and wondered if the hanging tree was strong enough to hold a double neck-stretching party. The thought made what passed for a smile come into Slade's face.

Eleven

Dawn on the third day found Lazarus red-eyed and feet hurting like hell. He smiled thinly thinking of the number of times he would have given half his pay to be able to get off his horse and stretch his legs. As he chewed his last piece of jerky, washing it down sparingly with a few drops of his rapidly diminishing water supply, he tried to think things out. He had to try and figure out some plan of action or he would end up dead or at the best, loco. And that could make him careless. Easy prey for the Apache or bounty-hunter or anyone who took a fancy to his Winchester or Dragoon.

Lazarus reckoned that he had put enough

distance between himself and the border to risk travelling by daylight. It would also be easier for him to see any Mexican village set back from the main trail. He could travel two, three days without food, more if he could stomach rattlers and lizards, but lack of water was something else. When the sun came up this wild land would bake. Without sufficient water he was already as good as dead.

By noon the blazing ball of fire that was the sun hung high in the fierce blue sky, pulling every bit of moisture out of Lazarus's body. He was almost tempted to throw away his war-bag and Winchester, their weight was slowing him down. But he had not lost all reason yet. Without them he would be as helpless as the old biblical prophets were walking about the wilderness, and they hadn't the Apache of hired killers to pester them, just the hunger and the thirst. He had to fight with himself to keep from drinking the last of his water he could hear swishing about in the canteen, but it was the fact that he kept promising himself a drink soon that enabled him to put one foot in front of the other. Drink it and his will to carry on would collapse.

When he first heard the sound of running water Lazarus thought that it was just a trick of his thirst-tortured mind. It sounded near but the burning red slits in a dirt-encrusted face could not focus properly. Desperately he poured the last of the water from his canteen over his face. It cleared Lazarus's vision enough for him to see the narrow trickling sheen of water among the rocks at the bottom of the wash. He had never been a praying man but he mumbled a few hallelujahs as he slid down to the water.

For a long time Lazarus sat with his bare feet in the water feeling that he was coming alive once again. Upstream the wash broadened, flattening the steep banks into gentle slopes. The goat came down the left hand slope to drink the water. Lazarus heard the sound of its bell as it drank. Quickly he slipped on his socks and boots and filled up his canteen. He slung his gear on his back so as to keep his hands free and walked up towards the goat, the Winchester held high across his chest and cocked. Belled goats meant people and people could be peaceable or hostile as he well knew.

Lazarus came out of the wash on the same side as the goat had come from and saw the old Mexican. He was busy repairing a stone wall behind which Lazarus could hear the sound of more goats. To the left of the goat-pen was a small growing patch, melons and corn, beyond that a single-storeyed adobe building whose

55

walls were pock-marked with age. Alongside the living-house were two part-timber, part-stone smaller buildings that Lazarus reckoned to be storage barns. He kicked at the soil with the toe of his boot and watched the dust spirals rise. He noticed the bowed back of the old man as he struggled to put a heavy stone into place.

The bent back of a near broken-spirited man wasting a lifetime trying to scratch an existence out of a dust-bowl. The Mexican worked bare-footed, bareheaded, saintlike in a land of the devil. Lazarus felt that he could have been back in Minnesota. It could have been his own father he was watching. Some of the iron went from his soul. The old man stopped working as Lazarus came walking up towards him. A face as worn and furrowed as the land about crinkled even further in a smile.

'Welcome to my home, Senor.'

Senor, thought Lazarus. It was the first time in his life he had been called Mister and he'd had to come to a foreign land to be paid that respect.

'*Gracias*, Senor...er,' he replied.

'Silveyra.'

'Brown,' said Lazarus and almost naturally he added, 'Here, let me finish the wall off. You sit yourself down a spell.'

Lazarus laid his gear on the ground and took

56

off his jacket and shirt. The old man gazed in awe at the broad-shouldered muscular torso.

'They feed you well in America, no, Senor Brown?'

Lazarus grinned back at him. 'Not lately Senor Silveyra, not lately.'

Lazarus worked on the wall until his body glistened with sweat. It was a long time since he had used his brains and hands for peaceable purposes. The satisfaction of it made him forget about the threats and the dangers that could be building up for him back along the trail. He placed the last stone in place and stood back and examined his work.

'*Bueno*, Senor Brown,' he heard the old man say.

Lazarus nodded in satisfaction. 'Not bad at that, Senor Silveyra, considering it's a while since I did farm work.'

He saw that there was a young girl, about eighteen or nineteen years old, standing alongside the old man. She wore a long white dress that scuffed the dust at her feet and her jet black hair reached to her waist. She gave Lazarus a shy half-smile reminding him of the faces of the madonnas he had seen in the Mexican places of worship in Texas. He then noticed the broken-legged doll the girl clutched tightly to her right hand.

'This is my granddaughter, Luisa, Senor.' He clapped his hands in mock anger and said,' 'Come, Luisa, food for our guest, pronto.' The girl smiled and turning on her heels she ran back into the house. 'It is not much, Senor Brown, a little cheese and bread and wine, but you are welcome to share it with us.'

'I've a few coffee beans left in my pack, Senor Silveyra,' Lazarus said.

'Coffee!' the old Mexican gasped. 'God truly favours the Silveyra household today.'

'And m'be a little tobacco,' grinned Lazarus.

'*Aie! Tobac?*' Senor Silveyra rocked on his feet and raised his arms skywards. 'All this happiness will break my heart.'

They sat and ate in the cool shadows of the storage barns. The girl, still with the fixed half-smile on her face, watched her grandfather eating then her gaze would turn to Lazarus and back again to her grandfather then back once more to Lazarus. Slowly, as if overcoming some inner nervousness she reached out a hand and touched Lazarus on the forearm. Her grandfather laughed.

'You are the first black man she has seen, Senor Brown.'

Lazarus smiled at the girl and took hold of her hands in his and rubbed them against his cheeks then showed her her palms.

58

'See, Luisa, clean. It doesn't rub off.'

The puzzling vacancy of Luisa's expression blossomed into a real smile.

Senor Silveyra's eyes gleamed with pleasure as he drew on his pipe.

'There are still some good times left even for us poor peons, Senor Brown,' he said contentedly.

Lazarus, watching Luisa feeding the goats, said, 'Do the Apache not bother you, Senor Silveyra?' He nodded towards Luisa. 'A young girl, easy prey for an Apache buck.'

'What can trouble the Apache here, Senor Brown? My son, Luisa's father, left the farm two years ago to seek his fortune in Mexico City. I have not heard from him since. An old man, nearing the grave, and a girl who is sick in the head cannot be any great prize even for the most bloodythirsty bronco. Even the Apache show compassion to those so afflicted. Sometimes a war band will come to water their ponies but that is all.' The old man puffed at his pipe, lost in his memories. Almost as an afterthought he said, 'She has been that way since birth, only her body has grown.'

'You have more than I have, Senor Silveyra,' said Lazarus. 'You have land and a loving granddaughter. I only have hope. What you can see is all that I own. I must find work soon.

I have been told that there is an Americano, a Senor Amos Bismark, who owns a big ranch several days' travel from here, who hires men.'

'That is true, Senor Brown,' the old man told him. 'The Hacienda Torrea-de-Carros hires many people. Senor Bismark is a good man. But to get to the rancheria you will have to cross the desert.' Senor Silveyra shrugged his shoulders. 'It will be very hard to do so on foot.'

'M'be so,' replied Lazarus. 'But I must try it. I can't go back.'

The old man knocked his pipe out on the ground. 'There is work to be done, Senor Brown. The water in the stream is drying up, the spring just below the far ridge must be blocked by stones again.'

Lazarus got to his feet. 'I'll go and check the spring out. It'll give me a chance to see what kind of land I'm heading into. Tell Luisa that when I get back I'll make her a new doll. It's the least I can do for the food you gave me, and the pleasure of your company.'

Senor Silveyra smiled his gratitude. 'She will be pleased, Senor Brown. She does not get many presents.'

Twelve

Macabe, in keeping in with his trade, sat at a table in the darkest corner of the cantina sipping slowly at what passed for genuine gringo whisky south of the Rio Grande. He was a man of the shadows, a killer who struck from out of the darkness on the unwary and the unexpecting. It was as he opined, the big nigra hadn't been in Coahati so he could still be on foot. Within forty miles of this mangy-dog town a man would be hard pushed to find himself a woman let alone a horse. Macabe grinned to himself. Slade's gold was already as good as spent.

He cast a leering look at the girl dancing on the table-top near the bar to the accompaniment of shouts and handclaps from about half a dozen drinkers. As she spun round, heels clacking like repeater rifle shots, her dress swirled waist-high and he feasted his eyes on brown smooth-skinned thighs. His tongue flickered over his lips in eager anticipation as the longing in his groin became an almost unbearable ache. He debated with himself whether or not he should stay on in Coahati another night so that he could satisfy that longing.

But it was a big, wild land out there and he didn't reckon to give the nigra any more of a lead than he already had. Not for a dollar whore. With Slade's bounty in his pocket he could get the fanciest and the sweetest piece of ass in the whole of Texas.

Macabe left town by way of the main trail. He had been this way before when he had ridden with a bunch of border cattle-lifters so he knew that away from the main trail there was only bad Indians and bad water. Suicide for a man on foot.

It was early afternoon when Macabe reached the house of Fernando Silveyra. He eased himself out of the saddle and without a by your leave he drank his fill from the goatskin that hung on the shaded wall of the hut. Macabe did not believe in the social graces of the border regions that obliged a traveller to ask the owner of the land he was on if he could step down and drink. He reckoned that custom did not apply to greasers.

Fernando, from his doorway, watched him drinking. This man was different to the black man. He had lived too long in a hard land not to recognize the wolfish shifty-eyed look of a *mal hombre*, a bad one.

'Hey, Mex!' Macabe called out. 'Has a big nigra passed through here?'

The old man had sensed that the black man had been running away from something or someone but whatever he had done he did not deserve to be placed in the hands of this man. A man who had not even found time to see to his horse's needs. He shook his head in puzzlement.

'Nigra? No *comprende*, Senor.'

'Nigra...black man, yuh bean-brain,' snarled Macabe. 'Ah picked up his tracks way back.'

'No, Senor,' replied Fernando firmly. 'You are the only traveller to visit my humble house.' He shrugged his shoulders resignedly. 'We are poor, Senor. What could we offer a traveller?'

'What do yuh mean, we?' questioned Macabe. Alarmed he pulled out his gun. 'Is there someone back there?' and pushed past the old man to enter the hut.

The old man put his hands on Macabe's chest.

'No, Senor,' he pleaded. 'Do not enter. My granddaughter, she is washing herself.'

'Granddaughter!' Macabe's blood temperature began to rise. 'Outa my way, old man,' and struck at him with his gun. Fernando gasped with pain and fell to the ground, blood

63

flowing freely from a gash in his forehead.

Macabe stepped into the room and Luisa turned at the sound of his footsteps, towelling her long black hair. Macabe stood, slack-jawed, gazing at the tight young breasts, water dripping off their proud tips. The burning ache set up in his loins again. Slade's gold would have to wait. He walked across to her, right hand busy at his flies.

'It ain't gonna hurt, Senorita,' he mouthed thickly. 'Well, m'be just a bit at first...'

The smile of welcome began to fade from Luisa's face when she saw that he was not the black man. Some inner instinct told her to cover her nakedness and she lowered the towel to hide her breasts. Concern and bewilderment replaced the smile. She had only a child's comprehension of things and happenings. She knew that the good things brought smiles, the bad, pain and tears. The tall black man had been good. He made her laugh. The feelings she got off this man were different. He did not make her smile. He must be bad. He even had a bad smell. Luisa could not reason what this bad man wanted from her. Her uncertainties and fears were mirrored in her wild staring eyes. Where was her grandfather and the kindly black man? She felt the bad man's hand on her flesh. It was sweaty and sticky and made her skin itch. The hand tore the towel away and Luisa screamed in pure terror.

Macabe struck her a vicious back-handed blow across the face. In a daze of pain and shock Luisa was conscious of being picked up and carried over to her cot. The bad feeling was much worse. It froze her mind and body into a rigid unresisting numbness. From the depths of the blankness she felt the weight of the man on top of her then heard herself scream again as a stabbing pain tore at her body.

Macabe came out into the sunlight, fastening up his pants. If only the little bitch had struggled a bit he thought, it would have made it more interesting. But it had eased him, made him forget about the whore in Coahati. He could now concentrate fully on trailing the black and earn his gold and spend it on dames that really knew what a grown man wanted.

Senor Silveyra shakily picked himself up and staggered into the hut. In the cot he saw a silent, unmoving bundle. For one fearful moment he thought that Luisa was dead. Then he heard a low moaning sound. Bending over her he could see the blood and bruises on her breasts and thighs.

'Madre Dios!' he sobbed as he crossed himself. With tears of pity and compassion in his eyes he gently covered her nakedness with

a blanket. He ran outside shouting at Macabe as the bounty-hunter rode across the wash.

'*Gringo bastardo!*' he yelled. Then he beat at his chest with his fists in angry frustration at his helplessness to avenge the ravishing of his granddaughter as tears of rage flooded down his face.

From the hillside Lazarus saw the horseman splashing across the wash. He dropped down on one knee and lined up the Winchester on the rider, keeping him in the sights until he disappeared over the rise. He waited several minutes before moving down to the hut. When he did, the rifle was held across his middle ready for snap-shooting from the hip. The rider could be the goat, drawing him into the open, for another man lying in ambush to pick him off.

He heard the old farmer shouting and forgetting his caution ran to him. Senor Silveyra gripped his arms tightly.

'It's Luisa, Senor Brown, that…that animal has defloro…what you say…deflowered her…'

Lazarus's face hardened. 'Don't you fret none, Senor Silveyra. If it's the last thing I do that raping bastard will pay for his pleasure. But first I must go and see Luisa.'

Lazarus sat at the head of the cot and smiled at Luisa. Luisa stared back at him, eyes wide but unseeing, still shocked and numbed by her ordeal. He took one of her hands in his, talking softly to her as he did so. Slowly Lazarus felt a pressure on his hand as Luisa began to grip tighter. Then the tears began to flow and Luisa's body shook with her sobs. Lazarus held her hand until at last she fell asleep, exhausted. Only then did he get up from the cot. Senor Silveyra, who had been a silent watcher said,

'You are a *bueno hombre*, a good man, Senor Brown. You know how to comfort people.'

'Like your family, Senor,' Lazarus said, 'my family had a lot of need for comfort and we could only get it from ourselves. I had to comfort my mother when my father died, comfort my brothers and sisters when she died. Oh yes, Senor,' his voice became bitter, 'I know how to bring comfort all right and as sure as hell that bastard who did this to Luisa is going to need a hellava lot of comforting after I'm finished with him.'

'Be careful, Senor,' the old man told him. 'Do not put yourself in danger for our sakes. That pig was trailing you.'

'Was he now?' Lazarus's fearsome grin made the old man mentally cross himself and he almost felt pity for the raper of his granddaughter when the big negro caught up with him.

'There is a way, beyond the goat-pen, that leads over the hills. If you travel fast, Senor Brown, you will get ahead of your hunter.'

Lazarus stopped and turned just before the track slipped over the first rise. He saw the old man still standing there and raised his hand in a farewell gesture. The old man waved his in acknowledgement there was another burden for Senor Silveyra's aged back to shoulder, the raping of his granddaughter and its possible outcome. The iron came back into Lazarus's soul.

Thirteen

Lazarus ran in a long, loping, ground-eating stride, his eagerness to get his hands round the gunman's throat making him ignore the weight of his warbag and the Winchester tugging at his shoulders.

The track steepened, cutting across hogback ridges, forcing the sweat out of Lazarus, making him drop into a hands-and-knees scramble. But his hatred for the man made him keep the heart-pounding pace going. At last the ground began to fall away and pausing to get his breath Lazarus saw through the timber-line the thin blaze of the trail. There was no sign of a rider on the long stretch he could see.

Lazarus dropped low just before he broke onto the trail. A quick reading of the ground showed no sign of any fresh horse tracks. The gunman was still between him and the old man's place. He moved on slower now. There was still plenty of cover but it would not do to take unnecessary risks. The man could be closer than he thought. Lazarus saw the horse first, tethered a little way back from the trail. Macabe was sitting beside a small smokeless fire.

Lazarus stepped into the open, pistol in his hand. The click of the hammer being cocked made Macabe whirl round but stayed the hand that was reaching for the rifle at his feet. Lazarus gave him a mirthless grin.

'You'll never make it, mister. Just blink an eyelid and I'll blow your head clean off. And I don't want you to die that easy. I want you to feel pain, like Luisa did.' Lazarus sheathed his gun. 'Now get onto your feet and show me how tough you are when you're facing a man.'

Macabe's death's-head face gave a fiend's grin as he stood up. His right hand flashed to his boot top and when it came up Lazarus saw the glint of steel in it.

'Ah'll cut yuh, yuh black sonavabitch,' his voice taking on a note of triumph. 'Ah'll cut yuh and deliver yuh tuh Slade in pieces.' He moved in closer to Lazarus, all the while cursing and slashing at the air in front of him with the knife.

Lazarus watched the knife hand like a hawk as he slowly side-stepped around Macabe, forcing the gunman to follow him. A mouth fighter, he thought. When they had to fight at anything like even odds they still had to bad-mouth their opponents to bolster up their own courage. He feinted with his left hand as though making a grab for the knife. Macabe grinned confidently and slipped under Lazarus's arm and with his own outstretched he lunged for Lazarus's belly. The killing spot. Where a knife could slip in hilt deep without meeting any resistance. A quick downward slash and a man could watch his own guts spill out. Just for that few nerve-shrieking seconds before he died.

Lazarus twisted his body away from the blade and brought up his right leg, fast and hard. Macabe's forearm snapped with a crack as loud as a pistol discharge and his breath left his body in one piercing scream of agony; and the knife flew away in a shining arc. Macabe, face yellowed in pain, stumbled into Lazarus.

Lazarus stepped back and swung his right fist. The blow caught Macabe full in the face, smashing his nose into a bloody mash of bone and gristle. The further pain put out the lights for Macabe and Lazarus gave a grunt of satisfaction as the gunman collapsed to the ground.

Slowly Macabe came to in a pain-filled world. He put his good hand to his face and felt the stickiness of blood and spongy flesh where his nose had once been.

'Yuh mean black bastard, yuh've marked me for life!' His voice was only a wheezing croak.

Lazarus grinned down at him. 'Ain't it the truth? But I wouldn't sit there too long chatting, it's a long walk back to Texas.'

'Yuh ain't gonna make me walk?' Macabe whined. 'Mah busted arm will stiffen up before ah get tuh a doc. Mah face...'

'That's your tough luck,' interrupted Lazarus. 'But I've need of your horse.'

Macabe struggled painfully to his feet, face twitching in fear.

'It'll be murder leaving me out here on mah own, yuh black bastard.'

'How would you have left me if things had turned out different?' replied Lazarus. 'I've left you a canteen of water, you won't feel like eating for a spell. Now just in case you're still mean enough to go back to the old man's place and take it out on him on the girl I'm going to light a fire, one with plenty of smoke. Out there,' Lazarus pointed with his chin to the hills, 'are the Apache, crawling all over the place. Apart from being right bloodthirsty they're also mighty curious. They'll be down here like the hounds of hell to see what all the smoke's about and they'll pick up your trail in no time at all.'

'T'aint right setting those red butchers on me,' cried Macabe.

'It might'n be right but it's justice,' answered Lazarus. He began to toss green wood onto the fire and fan it into flames. 'You're wasting time, white man.'

He swung up onto Macabe's horse. Macabe grabbed at his legs. Lazarus pushed his boot into the crimson smear of a face. The gunman yelled and fell away. On his way through the trees Lazarus picked up the Winchester and his warbag then gave the horse its head. He wanted to be well away from Macabe when his retribution came. Macabe's curses died away in the distance.

Macabe, half-dead on his feet, stumbled on. Every step he took sent waves of agony over his body. His broken nose had started to bleed again, filling his mouth with blood. As he spat it out to clear his throat so that he could breathe he thought of the different ways he would kill the big nigra. He would come back and hunt him down even if he'd only one arm and half a face and he would do it for just the pleasure. The black bastard's talk about the Apache had been all bluff. He'd not seen hide nor hair of them.

The trail led across the bed of an arroyo. Macabe climbed up the far bank, cursing with pain as the brush pulled at his broken arm. Just back from the edge they were waiting for him. Three of them, mounted on small shaggy ponies. Macabe turned and slid down the bank in a flurry of dust and stone, sobbing hysterically in bowel-moving fear, the pain of his arm and face forgotten. At the bottom stood the fourth Apache. The point of his lance pricked at Macabe's chest. Grinning he prodded him back up to the rim of the arroyo. When they smelt him the other Apache laughed as well.

It took a long time for Macabe to die. He lost the use of his vocal cords long before that happened. When the Apache left the arroyo the blackened, still smouldering thing that hung over the dead embers could hardly be recognized as a human being.

Fourteen

The stars were still visible in the sky when Lazarus began his journey across the desert. Senor Silveyra had said that he would find that the trail met up with a wide arroyo running north and south before he hit the desert and that if he dug deep enough into the sand at the bottom of the wash, and the saints smiled on his efforts, he would find a little water. The saints had shown their pleasure. The water was brackish but before the day was out Lazarus reckoned that it would taste as sweet as any he had drunk.

Both he and his horse drank their fill. He ate the cheese and bread Senor Silveyra had insisted he take, in exchange for the coffee and tobacco, and topped up his canteen. He made a final check on his gear, making sure that it was securely tied on, a lost canteen of water could mean disaster, and rode out of the wash and onto the desert. The next source of water he would see would be at the Hacienda Torrea-de-Carros. The trail was well defined, even by starlight, so Lazarus had no fears that he could wander off and get himself lost in the desert.

The sun came up fast, steaming away the chill night mist. Then came the heat. Hell's very own furnace it seemed to Lazarus. Still the horse soldier, he dismounted when he judged that he had ridden an hour, wet a cloth and wiped the caked sand from the horse's muzzle, then squeezed the remainder into its mouth, the horse neighing its appreciation. Probably the first kind deed it had had done to it thought Lazarus. Taking a mouthful of water himself he set off walking, leading the horse, for ten minutes. It was only then that he felt the full fierceness of the sun, making his walk to the old Mexican's farm seem like an afternoon stroll.

The old Mexican had been right. A man on foot, carrying all his gear, would never make it. Only an Apache or a Comanche would have a fair chance of reaching the other side. The sun, reflecting from the stony sand, raised a shimmering heat-haze that restricted his vision so that he could not see the mountains that Senor Silveyra had told him would mark his journey's end.

On his third spell of walking, a trail coming up from the south joined his trail and from now on the way was deeply grooved by the passage of heavy wagons. Any doubts that Lazarus might have had about people living on the far side of this hell-hole vanished. This must be the main supply route to the Hacienda Torrea-de-Carros. Several miles past the junction of the trails the desert began to break up as though slashed by some gigantic knife and Lazarus could only see from one dip to the next rise ahead of him.

Coming up to one rise Lazarus heard a sudden burst of gunfire. He pulled up his horse and listened. At least six guns he calculated and by its deep booming crack, one of them a heavy calibre long gun. A real battle was taking place over the next ridge. Something he didn't want to take part in. He was carrying enough trouble and worries without going seeking them out. If he could he'd skirt round whoever was doing the shooting and pick up the trail further along.

He gently knee'd his horse forward to the ridge and dismounted. Keeping low, his rifle off his shoulders and in his hands, he peered over the edge. The trail ran down a steep mesquite and brush dotted slope, levelled off on the flat then led across a broad salt-pan. A hundred and fifty yards or so along the flat Lazarus saw a wagon, one rear wheel off, lying on its side with some of its load spilled on the desert floor. He could see no sign of its team.

76

He counted two guns firing on the wagon from a gully ahead of it and two more, left and right of him halfway down the gradient. Three guns were at the wagon returning the ambusher's fire, one of them the big-sounding long gun. Lazarus quickly changed his mind about keeping out of trouble. The wagon could only be hauling supplies to the Hacienda. If he could help the three at the wagon to rout their attackers it would be an in for him.

Lazarus slung his rifle back onto his shoulders and ran back to his horse and drew out the bounty-hunter's rifle, then hurried back up to the rim-line and took a closer look at the situation.

The best way to help would be to put the two riflemen below him out of action. Then the way to the wagon was open. Lazarus could see the man to his left, kneeling behind a rock, quite clearly. The other one he couldn't exactly pinpoint. He was well hidden in the brush. The rifleman behind the rock brought up his rifle for an animal shot at the wagon. Lazarus fired first.

The shot changed the expression on the gunman's face into one of disbelief and agonizing pain as he slumped back against the rock, sinking lower into the ground until finally he lay still. Lazarus ducked down as a shot from the man in the brush screeched over his head. He now had a fight on his hands. The advantage of surprise had gone.

Lazarus risked another quick look over the edge and drew another shot, showing that the gunman wasn't about to be easily surprised. But he had seen, further along to his right, just before the bank steepened, where a man could, if he took it carefully and didn't set off a landslip and go ass over tip and break his neck, get down and behind the gunman, regaining the ace card of surprise. There was a lot of ifs, but it was a chance.

Lazarus laid his rifle over the rim and fired three quick rounds in the general direction of the gunman. Just to let him know that he was still here on the ridge. He heard two shots in answer as he drew back down. The man in the brush was anything but asleep. Lazarus ran below the ridge to where he judged the place was he had picked out for his descent. Snakelike, he slipped over the rim, keeping a wary eye and ready gun on the gunman's position. With the friction of his buttocks and heels holding him back against the run of the gradient he knee-jerked his way down.

Lazarus reckoned that he was almost opposite the gunman's position and he stopped

78

his inching downwards for a closer look into the brush to see if he could pick out his target. Suddenly the bankside beneath him slipped away, hurtling him downward on his back, arms flailing wildly, in a cloud of dust and rattling stones. The Sharps on his shoulders dug into the ground, acting as a brake, swung him round, leaving him, choking and half-blinded with dust, broadside across the slope. Lazarus struggled like a fly caught in a spider's web to get hold of the Winchester lying several feet away from his outstretched hands while below him the landslip roared its way to the floor of the arroyo.

He stopped his efforts as he saw the gunman come out of the brush and braced his body for the impact and the pain as the man aimed his rifle. The deep boom of the big gun at the wagon ended that fear. The sledgehammer blow of its heavy charge flung the gunman back into the bush like a child might throw away a rag doll. Lazarus scrambled to his feet, picked up the Winchester, and not worrying about broken limbs, in a sliding run reached the flat.

'Hullo, the wagon!' he yelled. 'I'm coming on in!'

Weaving and ducking he dashed towards the wagon. He saw hands pulling aside a box to make an opening for him and the guns under the guns under the wagon drummed out their loads to give him covering fire. The last few yards Lazarus took at a flying run, landing him up against the wagon side with a crash that jar-red every bone in his body.

'Welcome, pilgrim. Much obliged tuh yuh for cutting down the opposition and fur giving me a chance to blast that no-good sonavabitch road agent tuh kingdom come or wherever the Good Lord intends him tuh end up.'

It was a whipcord-thin, grey-whiskered, elderly man wearing a faded serape, busy ram-ming a fresh shell into the breech of a long-barrelled single-shot Sharps buffalo gun that spoke.

'Think nothing of it,' replied Lazarus. 'That museum piece you're holding got me out of a mess of trouble back there. I was heading for the Hacienda-Torrea-de-Carros, I heard that they're hiring there, when I heard the shoot-ing.'

'Yuh've already started earning yuhr pay... Mister...er?'

'Brown, Lazarus Brown, sir.'

'I'm Amos Bismark, boss of the Hacienda.' The old man reached out a hand and Lazarus gripped it in a firm honest handshake. The rancher grinned. 'That villainous character

80

under the big hat is mah chief vaquero, Miguel, and this young thing here is mah daughter, Elizabetta.'

The solemn-faced Mexican gave Lazarus a curt nod and went back to peering along the barrel of his Winchester. The third person under the wagon was worth a longer look in spite of bullets thucking into the wagon boards. She wore a short blue dress and hand-worked soft leather leggings that exposed a lot of brown smooth flesh. Her jet-black hair was fixed high, Spanish style held up by a golden-coloured comb from her small-boned face. Lazarus watched her hands as she deftly slipped new loads into her rifle. He had men in his troop that were a lot slower and clumsier reloading on the shooting ranges. She handled the Winchester easily and confidently as another girl might handle knitting. She smiled at Lazarus and he thought that it was one of the sweetest things he had seen.

'Welcome to Hacienda Torrea-de-Carros, Senor Brown.' Her voice was soft and warm. Like her body.

'At first I thought that it was the Apache that were doing the shooting,' said Lazarus.

The girl and her father looked across at each other and laughed. Even the grim-faced Miguel smiled.

'Apache, naw, Mr Brown,' said Amos Bismark. 'They're no-good white trash from across the border. Capable of anything but earning an honest living. They nearly caught us out when the wagon wheel came off but Miguel spotted them and we managed tuh fort up under the wagon.' The rancher heaved himself up. 'Well that's enough socializing. Ah think that it's time we took the war tuh those two drygulchers up ahead. They'll not have the stomach for a real fight now that they've discovered that the hoped-for pickings are not so cheap as they thought. Ah'll take that spare Winchester yuh're carrying, Mr Brown, and yuh and me will go out turkey shootin'. Yuh two make sure they keep their heads low.'

Lazarus rolled out from under the wagon as the two covering rifles opened up. Their rapid concentrated fire raised a curtain of dust several feet high along the rim that sheltered the gunmen. He got to his feet and straightened up and brought his own gun into action, firing single shots into the dust. No return fire from the gunmen came his way. It was like walking forward under a wall of steel.

The guns stopped firing from the wagon as Elizabetta and Miguel paused to reload. The dust began to break up in the light wind and Lazarus saw a moving indistinct shape. The gunman was getting to hell out of it. He aimed the Sharps and pulled off the remainder of its loads. He heard a scream of pain and the sound of a heavy object rolling down into the arroyo.

'I think I've got him, Mr Bismark!' he shouted.

Amos Bismark raised his rifle above his head.

'Likewise, Mr Brown!'

Lazarus moved into the arroyo slowly, Dragoon out and cocked just in case the gunman was playing possum, but his aim had been true. The man lay in a crumpled heap on the floor of the wash. He walked along the edge, closing in on Mr Bismark who was moving in to join him when a voice said,

'Hold it there, nigra. Just act naturally. Don't warn that old bastard or I'll plug yuh now. Ah want him closer so that ah can get yuh both without those two at the wagon getting a bead on me.'

Lazarus cursed under his breath. It could only be the horse guard. With all the shooing going on they would be frightened in case their horses spooked and ran off into the desert. He placed the man just behind him, a little to his left. If he turned fast enough he could get one shot off before he was gunned down. It was worth the attempt. He couldn't let Elizabetta's father walk into a trap and get himself killed. Lazarus didn't want to see her sweet smiling end so soon in her life. The gunman must have read his thoughts or more likely saw his back tense up as he prepared to swing round shooting.

'Don't try it, boy. Yuh'll get it soon enough. When that...' the voice suddenly cut off in a throaty gurgle.

Lazarus risked a look over his shoulder and caught a glimpse of the gunman's head and shoulders, and the two feathered sticks protruding from his back as he fell on to his face. One moment there had only been the two of them, then, their ponies high-stepping it up the sandy bank, they were all around him. Near enough to smell their tangy woodsmoke body-sweat and feel the heat coming off the ponies' steaming flanks. Close enough to freeze him rigid with fear. Their ponies brushed against him as the war-daubed faces and stone-hard eyes looked him over.

Faintly Lazarus heard Amos Bismark shout, 'Don't yuh fret none, Mr Brown, they're friends of ours.'

The old rancher pushed his way through the press of horses, Indian-talking to their riders until he stood alongside Lazarus.

He grinned. 'Ah swear, Mr Brown, yuhr face

84

nearly turned white.'

Lazarus swallowed hard before he could speak. 'I ain't been this close to them before without being backed up by a troop of cavalry blazing away with carbines.'

'Ah'll admit that they look mighty mean when they're dressed up in their Sunday best,' replied Mr Bismark. 'But as ah said, they're friends of mine...well more than friends. That hatchet-faced old cuss with the eagle feathers head-dress is Elizabetta's uncle and ah reckon there must be at least three or four second cousins in the bunch as well.' Mr Bismark spoke again, in what seemed to Lazarus's ears a series of doglike barks and growls, to the Apache chief.

The chief looked in his direction and nodded to Amos Bismark.

'Ah told him yuh were mah friend, Mr Brown, so the Warm Springs Apache should not bother yuh if yuh bump into them again on yuhr travels. But ah would advise yuh tuh steer clear of any other Apache bands...Mah blood ties don't stretch that fur.'

He saw the look of surprise still on Lazarus's face. 'Yes, Mr Brown, ah'm what the Texans call a squaw-man. Elizabetta's grandpappy on my wife's side was Chief Santos. He got himself killed in a brush with some horse soldiers. So like yuh, ah know what it's like tuh be hounded by white men.'

Amos Bismark spoke some more Apache and the war band split up. A party rode down to the wagon, the rest riding east along the trail.

'They're riding out tuh round up the mule-team,' Mr Bismark told Lazarus. 'They broke loose and high-tailed it when the shootin' started. The others are giving us a hand to fix the wagon.

'They just like us, Mr Brown,' the old rancher said as they followed the Apache down to the wagon. 'In fact in some things better than us. Ah've never known an Apache go back on his word but ah certainly know a passel of so-called white folk that's never kept theirs. They see things more clearly than us lying, twisting, cheating whites. Yuh're either their friends or their enemies and that don't depend on the colour of yuhr skin. All they want is to be able tuh live their own way of life, as they've done so fur the past three hundred years. Yuh wouldn't think that was a lot to ask fur, Mr Brown, would yuh? But the land-grabbing whites won't let them.'

With the help of the Apache and Lazarus's great strength they got the wheel fixed back on by the time the rest of the war band returned with the mules. The team was hitched up and the wagon was ready for rolling. Lazarus told Mr Bismark that he would go back for his horse and catch them up along the trail. When he did the Apache had gone. There was no sign of Elizabetta's uncle or her wild country cousins. Not even a wisp of trail-dust to mark their going. Behind him the carrion birds stopped their impatient squawking and circling and dropped like lead-shot to the floor of the desert and their unexpected meal.

Fifteen

As the wagon neared the Candelarias, green took over from the browns and the reds of the desert, slowly at first. Then came the tall Alomas, the sun-flashing water, then the longer grass and the cattle. Beyond the water ran the long stone wall that enclosed the land of the Hacienda Torrea-de-Carros.

The wagon drove through the main gateway in the wall but Lazarus still found it a fair ride before the main buildings of the rancho, nestling in a small sheltered valley, came in sight. The big house was a long, rectangular, one-storeyed, white-plastered building. Its windows were iron-barred and could be further strengthened by the closing of thick wooden shutters; loopholed for defensive fire by its occupants in case of attack.

'Some fort you have here, Mr Bismark,' Lazarus said.

'There was a need for it when the old Don ran the place,' Amos Bismark grinned. 'He hadn't Apache relations. They came swarming over the Candelarias in what the old Texans called Apache moon nights. Taking what they could, burning what they couldn't. It's taken me a long time tuh get things built up again. It's a constant fight against the desert. No wonder the old Don sold up and moved south. The desert and the Apache would be too much fur any man tuh take on.'

The wagon pulled up alongside some outbuildings and Elizabetta jumped down from the wagon and ran back to the big house. Lazarus dismounted and helped Miguel and several vaqueros who had come out of the crew's quarters to unload the wagon.

'The men will show yuh where to wash up, Mr Brown,' Amos Bismark said. 'Then come up tuh the big house for a welcome to the ranch dinner.' Noticing Lazarus's hesitation in replying he growled, 'Don't yuh like eating with a squaw-man?'

88

Lazarus shook his head. 'Nothing like that, Mr Bismark. It's just that it's not every day I'm invited to share a white man's table. The last invite I got from a white man was to kick my legs under his hanging tree.' Whether it was the impression the sweet-smiling Elizabetta had made on him or just his stubborn pride that would not let him lie about the reason of his being below the border, and the fact that he wanted the old rancher to know that he could have hired himself a heap of trouble as well as a new hand, he found himself telling Amos Bismark the full story. The hanging, the shootings, the desertion—even Slade's bounty-hunter.

Amos Bismark listened to it all in silence, then after Lazarus had finished he blurted out, 'Well ah'll be damned...Jason Slade. Ah thought the old bastard had long since died.'

'Did you know him, Mr Bismark?' Lazarus asked.

The old rancher gave a mirthless laugh. 'We were as close as brothers one time. We became men together. After we whupped Santa Anna in '36 we stayed on in Texas as pardners, to build the biggest cattle ranch in the country. For two stony-broke kids we sure had grand ideas. Yuh might think that Texas is a wild place now, Mr Brown, but when me and Jason

Slade started out it was hell's own place. There were more land and cattle deals settled by a Colt pistol than all the fancy back-east lawyers ever did.' Amos Bismark paused. 'He'll never give up hunting for yuh, Mr Brown, not Jason Slade.'

'I knew he was a proud man,' said Lazarus. 'But I didn't think he could hate that long.'

Amos Bismark snorted. 'He's hated me nigh on twenty years and ah was one of his best friends...his only friend. As ah said, we started to build up the herd together. Jason was in a hurry to get tuh the top. What he wanted he took. Riding roughshod over everybody who gave him no for an answer. Ah didn't like his style so we split up, still more or less friends even tho' ah started building mah own brand. Slade got himself a wife, a nice Texas girl. But that didn't mellow him none. Ah got me a wife, an Apache girl, Elizabetta's mother. That shook Jason, stretched our friendship to the limit. Wouldn't come tuh see us, tho' his wife did.' Amos Bismark stopped as if recalling his thoughts and memories. 'It musta been in the fall of '59 when the final break came. It had been a bad year fur Indian raids, those Apache moon nights ah was telling yuh about. Ten or twelve war bands out, burning, killing and generally raising hell. Everybody had tuh fort up, excepting me. Slade's wife and his baby son were two of the victims. He'd always been a hard man but the killing of his wife and son turned him into a mean one. Gave orders that if that Indian-loving bastard, yuhrs truly, was seen on his land he had tuh be shot.' Amos Bismark's voice softened and the wiriness seemed to go out of his body. 'A month later my wife was raped and killed by so-called white men, like that bunch we met back there on the trail. So like yuh, Mr Brown, ah can take or leave white men. Now get yuhrself presentable and come tuh dinner at the big house. Elizabetta will be getting something special ready.' The old rancher's smile came back. 'She's got her grandpappy Chief Santos's fiery temper and she don't like guests not showing up. When she's roused that's something terrible tuh behold, Mr Brown.'

Sitting on the porch after they had finished eating, Amos Bismark asked Lazarus if he had ever worked cattle. Lazarus only half-heard him. His mind was still occupied with the thought of Elizabetta. She had looked fine in her range clothes under the wagon but at dinner, in a dress and the raven-black hair combed out, she was a vision that poor lonely dog soldiers, in barracks or on the plains, could hardly imagine in their dreams.

'Work cattle, did you say, Mr Bismark?' Lazarus smiled. 'I've eaten my way through a good size herd since I joined the Ninth but to be fair I can hardly tell one end of a longhorn from the other. If you want work that requires strength and not too much thinking then I'm your man.'

Amos Bismark grinned back. 'There's some rebuilding wanted on the north stretch of wall. The vaqueros can't manage it. Take them off their horses and away from the beef and they're lost. It'll be a good help if yuh can oblige, Mr Brown.'

'I would be pleased to help,' replied Lazarus. 'I've already had my hand in at wall building since I came south.'

'Good,' said Amos Bismark. 'Ah'll see tuh it that the wagon is loaded and a couple of peons come with yuh tuh help out.' The old man got up from his chair and knocked out his pipe. 'Ah'm off tuh bed. Ah ain't as young as ah used tuh be and one way and another its been a hectic day. See yuh in the mornin', Mr Brown, goodnight.'

Lazarus stood up also. 'Goodnight, Mr Bismark.' He turned his head as he heard the sound of light footsteps and the swishing of silk. Elizabetta stood in the doorway.

'I was wondering when you were coming

indoors, Father,' she said, mock angrily. 'There's a chill in the night air. Can't have you catching cold. You know how bad a patient you are.'

'Wimmin!' Amos Bismark growled as he walked past Lazarus. But Lazarus saw the old man's left eye wink. He waited until the rancher had gone inside before he thanked Elizabetta for the meal.

'It was our pleasure, Mr Brown. It was the least we could do for the help you gave us at the ambush.'

'Well...goodnight, Miss Bismark.'

'Elizabetta, Mr Brown. Miss Bismark makes me feel old.' And came that sweet smile again that made Lazarus feel like a callow, lovesick youth all the way to the crew's quarters and kept him awake most of the night.

Next day Lazarus and the peons were repairing the north wall of the Hacienda. He saw Elizabetta had waved a hand in greeting before she and her horse were lost against the backdrop of the foothills of the Candelarias. According to the peons, every day at the same hour the lady of the Hacienda would go for her ride and bathe in the fresh-running water-pool in the hills.

Lazarus, as he worked the plaster; imagined the slim bronzed body framed between the sun and the water. That, he sighed, would be a sight that most men would give their right arms to see. A peon shouting for more plaster put an end to such blissful thoughts.

The days that followed were hard working days for Lazarus. As Mr Bismark had said, there was still plenty of work to do on the ranch apart from rearing the stock. The desert had to be prevented from reclaiming the land again, the water, the life blood of the Hacienda, kept free-running. Here on the land of the Hacienda Torrea-de-Carros he could walk proud among proud men. Men like Amos Bismark who did not bend against the winds of bigotry and prejudice. He had only come south to protect his daughter.

In Texas a half-breed Indian girl, like a pretty negro one, would be considered easily available by any white horn-dog in the territory and Elizabetta wouldn't know or understand why it was so. On her father's land she could ride proud of both her races. Under the wagon she showed the stoic fearlessness of the Apache. At dinner in the big house, Elizabetta dressed and acted like any well-bred lady of the ranch. Yet she judged people like her father did and grand-pappy Santos had, not by the colour of their skins. And that made them the good days for Lazarus as well as the hard.

94

He did not know how Elizabetta felt about him. What she could see in him? What could he offer her? A strong back? That was the only thing he had of any value in the world. If that's all she wanted they'd be a long line of strong-backedmen stretching to the Rio Grande and beyond willing to pay court to her. Then Lazarus cursed himself for having such high-faluting and fancy thoughts. A hired hand sparking up to the boss's daughter, a black man at that. Even if it could be so he might have to leave the Hacienda at any time. How much control he had over his future depended on how mean Jason Slade was. The sooner he put such foolish romantic notions out of his mind the more restful he would sleep.

Sixteen

From his room window in the El Paso Cattle-man's Hotel Jason Slade looked out into the night, across the dark waters of the Rio Grande, and wondered how Macabe was faring. He'd had no word from the bounty-hunter since he had left the Lazy Y. No news is good news they said. But Slade, by experience a hard-headed realist, knew that no news often meant that the writer was dead.

He was a man that liked problems and mishaps sorted out quickly. Over the years it had grown into an obsession. A way of life. A long time ago it had taken time to get things straightened out. Wasted time. Holding him back from getting on with his dream of building the biggest cattle empire in the south-west. Now he had wealth and power he could sweep away any minor irritant or personal affront by a nod in the right quarter or a banker's cheque. The big nigra was an annoying loose end that niggled at his guts. Those of his enemies that he had not seen planted in Boot Hill or swinging from the hanging tree would be laughing behind his back at the thought of a nigra blue-belly twisting iron-man Slade's tail.

A knock at the door put an end to his ruminating. He strode across the room and opened it. A nondescript man with trail-dust still powdering his clothes stood in the hall.

'Mr Slade?' the man asked.

'Yes. What is it?' Slade replied irritably. 'Ah don't hire hands from hotel rooms. Mah foreman does that back at the Lazy Y.'

'Ah ain't come about no hiring, Mr Slade. It's about a big nigra ah heered yuhr interested in, willing to pay gold for news of his whereabouts ah also heerd.'

Slade did not let his interest show in his face. Since the announcement of the big hunt every saddletramp and bum in Texas had beat a trail to the Lazy Y ten feet wide to claim the bounty. They had seen the nigra in El Paso, Austin, Mexico City, even as far north as the trail towns on the Kansas plains. Finally he had told Ketch that he had to horsewhip the next man that stood on the porch of the big house and talked about sighting the nigra off the ranch.

'If the information is genuine ah'm willing tuh pay,' said Slade.

'Ah've just crossed the Rio Grande, Mr Slade. Been riding for a Mex cattle outfit the last six weeks. There was talk amongst the vaqueros that a Yankee, an Amos Bismark who owns a big spread up near the Candelarias, has a nigra working for him. To be fair, Mr Slade, ah don't rightly know whether Mr Bismark's nigra is the one yuhr after. Ah'm just telling yuh how ah heard it.'

Amos Bismark. Of course, Slade thought. Why the hell did I not think of him? What better place for a fugitive nigra but the ranch of an Indian-lover? He put his hand into his vest pocket and took out several gold pieces and handed them to the cow-hand.

'Ah'm much obliged tuh yuh, sir,' he told the man. 'If yuh ever need work mah spread is on the Brazos, up Fort Dodds way. If ah'm not there just tell mah foreman that ah sent yuh.'

The cow-hand touched his hat in thanks. 'I'll remember, Mr Slade. Hope it's the nigra yuh're after and yuh git him.'

After the cow-hand had left Slade sat down and lit a cigar. It's not every day a name mentioned can bring a man's whole life to mind, allowing the waters that had flowed under the bridge of time to come flooding back. Amos Bismark. It must be nearly twenty years since he last saw him and two, three, years before that when they first began to drift apart.

As young curly wolves, they had fought alongside old Sam Houston at San Jacinto, knocked the tar out of Santa Anna, sent him and the whole Mex army scuttling back across the Grande. Leaving Texas for the Texans to run and control. They had started building a joint spread together. Fighting Apache, Comanche and Mexs to hold on to their piece of land. He had lost count of the number of scars and hunks of lead their bodies had taken in saving each other's lives.

Then Amos Bismark disagreed with him on

the way things were going and started to set up his own brand. Just after that he'd got himself married. So did Amos. An Apache chief's daughter. That had galled him. The final straw that put an end to their friendship. He couldn't stomach having a squaw-man as a friend. Bismark had a half-breed daughter, she would be coming up to twenty now. If she was still alive. About the same age as his Tom would have been if he had not been lying there on the hill facing the Brazos along with his mother these past nineteen years. Then Amos sold his ranch and moved into old Mexico and ran cattle there on that fancy-sounding name the man from below the border had not mentioned, the Hacienda Torrea-de-Carros.

Slade gripped his chair hard. If Amos Bismark thought that their former friendship would stop him from hauling in the black he had another think coming. He wouldn't eat crow for any man. The cigar had been smoked out a long time before Slade called it a day and went to bed.

Seventeen

Both men got to their feet when Jason Slade
entered the inner office of the El Paso branch
of the Pinkerton Detective Agency. The tall
broad-shouldered man behind the desk reached
over and put out his hand.

'Ah, Mr Slade. I'm Robert T Jopling, officer
in charge of the agency and this is Agent Blake,
one of our operatives. We've just been discuss-
ing your case...Please sit down.'

The little fat clean-shaven man in funeral
black and yellow tan shoes nodded his head in
greeting. Slade got a smell of lavender water
as the eyes behind the wire-rimmed glasses gave
him a quick head-to-toe look. Jesus H Christ
he thought, is this one of the expert trackers
of wrongdoers that Mr Allan Pinkerton boasts
he has on his payroll? The disbelief must have
shown in his face for Robert T Jopling laughed
out loud.

'I know what you're thinking, Mr Slade, but
you're wrong. Why, Agent Blake has just
finished a successful operation in the Indian
Nations. Rounding up a band of murdering

road agents that had been plaguing the Wells Fargo stage line.'

Slade was still not convinced. Scented hair tonic and Jim Dandy shoes didn't somehow fit in with hunting down badmen in the Nations.

'Agent Blake will explain his plan of action, Mr Slade,' said Robert T Jopling.

Slade growled. 'Ah've still half a mind tuh go in and cut him out, Stonewall Jackson style. Eight or nine good men should do it.'

Once more Agent Blake fixed his short-sighted gaze on Slade. He smiled blandly and in a soft but firm voice he said,

'That would not be advisable, Mr Slade. Although you tell us that you have had intelligence from below the border that Mr Brown is or was working for the er...Indian-lover, Mr Amos Bismark, on the Hacienda Torrea-de-Carros, he might have been only working there to raise a grubstake and by now could have moved on. You'll be risking your neck for nothing. For there's the strong possibility that you could run into a bunch of Mr Bismark's Indian friends. Or the Rurales or a Regular Mexican Army patrol. Then you'll have a small war on your hands.'

Jason Slade squirmed in his chair.

'You say that it is over a month since Macabe, that was his name, wasn't it, left Coahati and he has not been seen or heard of since.'

Slade nodded.

Agent Blake clicked his tongue disapprovingly. 'That's the worst of using amateurs for real detective work.'

Slade got hotter under the collar.

'Macabe could be still trailing Brown of course,' continued Agent Blake. 'But it is my guess that he is dead, killed by Brown or the Apache or Mexican brigands, so we will have to assume that Brown knows, if he didn't already have a strong feeling that you would send someone after him, that he is still being hunted. He will be watching his back trail most carefully.'

'How the hell do yuh intend getting him out?' blurted out Slade.

The watery eyes behind the glasses gave Slade a pitying look.

'Why, we come in ahead of him, Mr Slade. If Mr Brown does move south he'll have to pass through Chihuahua City. That's where I'll start. If he's not been seen there I'll work my way up north, as a drummer selling cloth and geegaws to the ladies of the haciendas, especially those in the Hacienda Torrea-de-Carros. One way or another, Mr Slade, we'll find out if Mr Brown is still below the Rio Grande.'

'Then what will yuh do?' asked Slade. 'It's a long haul from there to Texas even without a prisoner tuh watch twenty-fou. hours a day.'

'We come south again, Mr Slade. I'll have two men as a back-up not too far away and at Chihuahua City there'll be a private stage waiting. Once we get over the border you can have a marshal ready to serve the warrant.'

Slade sat silent for a minute or two thinking it all over. Whorehouse perfume and fancy shoes or not the little fat dude certainly knew his business.

'It could work, it could just work, Mr Blake,' he said grudgingly.

Agent Blake got up from his chair. 'If we fail, Mr Slade, you can try your way.' A smile broadened his face. 'But remember what happened to Stonewall Jackson.'

Eighteen

Pinkerton Agent Blake stood at the end of the straggly line of 'dobe buildings that bore the fancy name of Bermejillo. From the last house stretched miles and miles of stony desert right up to the dark smudge of the Candelaria Mountains that covered the distant horizon. At their foothills was the Hacienda Torrea-de-Carros, the home of Amos Bismark, Slade's Indian-lover, and he hoped, where Lazarus Brown was. But all he knew for certain was that a negro had not been seen south of here. But each lead had to be checked out no matter how long it took.

Although the desert to his eyes and ears seemed silent and showed no sign of movement on its surface he had been told that an Apache war band was out there ready to jump any foolhardy traveller risking the trip to the Hacienda. Of course Agent Blake was well aware that it could be a rumour set about by the hotel-owner to stop him leaving so that he could screw a few more Yankee dollars out of his visitors. But he could not take that chance. His dude-like appearance and innocent simplicity might have fooled the badmen and bully boys of the Indian Nations but what he had heard about the ways of the Apache a glib tongue was of no use at all.

He and the two men he had brought to help him just in case Mr Brown proved awkward were staying at the one and only hostelry the town boasted. Three fresh horses had been hired, ready for moving at an hour's notice and the special stage was booked and waiting at Chihuahua City. Everything was in place for when the Apache called it a day and recrossed the Rio Grande. A shout of 'Senor' broke into Agent Blake's thoughts. He turned and waited until the Mexican came up to him. He recognized him as one of the cantina bartenders.

'A vaquero has ridden in from the Hacienda Torrea-de-Carros, Senor. He speak of the Apache moving north, back through the mountains, to Texas, and that there is a wagon following later today to pick up supplies for the Hacienda.'

'Good man,' replied Agent Blake. He handed the bartender a silver coin. The man touched his brow and with a 'Gracias, Senor' returned to the cantina.

Agent Blake smiled to himself. It was turning out even better than he'd dared hope. By tonight he should know for certain whether or not a black man was at the Amos Bismark hacienda.

Agent Blake, over the top of his newspaper, watched the two men come into the cantina. A tall straight-backed black man and an elderly wiry grey-bearded man who had the air of authority about him. Agent Blake tagged him as Amos Bismark. He drank up his coffee and casually got to his feet, folded up his newspaper and, just as relaxed, left the cantina. Once outside he hurried along to the hotel and spoke to one of his men who was sitting on the porch.

'We've hit paydirt, Ben. You and Tom get packed up...get to the horses. We should be on our way to Chihuahua City within the hour.'

Ben nodded in confirmation and went back inside the hotel. Agent Blake walked back into the cantina. Bismark and Brown were sitting at a table near the window. He strode across and sat down on the empty chair facing them.

He came straight to the reason for his interruption of their drinking before the two got over their surprise at his sudden appearance.

'I'm a Pinkerton agent and I've been instructed to escort one Lazarus Brown, negro, back to Texas where a warrant will be served by a United States marshal for the murder of three men.' He looked directly at Lazarus. 'I take it that you, sir, are the said Lazarus Brown.'

Lazarus made a move towards his hip. Agent Blake smiled coldly.

'Don't do anything foolish, Mr Brown.' With his left hand he slightly lifted the

106

newspaper that was draped over his right forearm and Lazarus glimpsed the snub-nosed pistol.

Lazarus still thought that the chance was worth it, a lot better odds than he would get in Texas at the hands of Jason Slade, but he felt Amos Bismark's knee press warningly against his so held back, trusting that the old man had an ace or two up his sleeve.

Amos Bismark gave Agent Blake a sneering look.

'A Pinkerton man, eh. Ah heerd it was just a high-falutin' name for a bounty-hunter.' He sniffed loudly. 'Tho' ah'll admit that yuh smell a mite sweeter, what with that fancy pomade on yuhr hair, than a back-shootin' no-good bounty-hunter.'

Agent Blake's face reddened with hurt pride.

'We agents work within the law, Mr Bismark,' he said angrily. 'We try to fetch our men back alive. I get no reward. Mr Brown here will have a fair trail in a court of law.'

'Slade's law, a boss-man's law,' replied Lazarus. 'How many black men will be on the jury, Mr Pinkerton man?'

'That has nothing to do with the Agency, Mr Brown. We...'

'But it has plenty tuh do with Lazarus,' interrupted Amos Bismark. 'It's his neck they want tuh stretch just because he killed three men in a fair fight after they had lynched his best friend. That's a queer sort of justice yuh Pinkertons subscribe tuh.'

Agent Blake did not answer him as over their shoulders he noticed a girl walking towards the table. His Pinkerton-trained mind quickly assessed her. Age about twenty, dark-haired, dressed in a pink dress, olive-skinned fine-boned face, possibly daughter of a well-to-do rancher. As the girl passed the table he gave her his best oily drummer smile.

'*Buenos dias*, Senorita.' The girl acknowledged his greeting with a fleeting smile. It was only then that Agent Blake got a good look at her eyes. They were not the soft warm eyes of a grandee's daughter. At the back of his mind an alarm bell rang. The girl went from his view and he focused all his attention back to the two men opposite him. And he wondered why that old goat, Amos Bismark, was smiling. Even the black man seemed to have relaxed. The bells rang louder.

'Now as I was saying...' Then he heard the girl say,

'Drop that pistol, fat man.'

Agent Blake cursed under his breath. He had been outfoxed by a slip of a girl. He risked a quick glance over his right shoulder. She was standing five or six feet away and it was any-thing but a slip of a gun she held in her hand. His methodical mind catalogued it as a .44 Colt. A small cannon, even from across the street. This close. Agent Blake swallowed hard and sweat began to roll down his moon face. Speed-ily he weighed up his options. His instincts told him that the two men facing him were the big-gest threat. But first he had to sweet-talk the girl into putting the pistol down while making sure that the two across the table did not make their play. He wondered why the bells had not stopped ringing.

'Now, young lady why don't...' The roar-ing boom of the big Colt stopped Agent Blake's sweet talk and drowned out the alarm bells. He let out a loud yelp of pain, like a hound dog being kicked unwarranted in the ribs, as a red-hot iron seared its way across the back of his gun hand. The pistol clattered onto the table top. Gingerly he removed the smouldering newspaper and saw the angry-looking weal beginning to drip red.

'She...she shot me...' he gasped. On his face was a look of pained astonishment.

Amos Bismark grinned back at him as he picked up the gun.

'She surely did, Mr Pinkerton-man, she sure-ly did.'

The girl came round to stand behind Amos and Lazarus. Through pain-blurred eyes Agent Blake saw that her eyes were now soft and brown like a young Spanish girl's should be. He suddenly remembered where he had seen her other look before. It was when he was crossing Texas, on his way to El Paso at some godforsaken army post on the Cimmaron, that he had seen several bronco Apache being brought in by a horse soldier patrol. They had had the same hard-eyed unblinking stare of pure hatred.

'This is mah daughter, Mr Pinkerton-man. Right purty, ain't she? But she's got a hair-trigger temper on account of grandpaw on her ma's side being a full-blood Apache war-chief. Now mah side of the family is peaceable folk. Why we'd walk a mile just tuh avoid a ruckus. But grandpaw Santos's kinfolk, well...when they tell yuh to do something yuh'd better do it quick, that's if yuh want tuh stay in one piece.'

White-faced, Agent Blake gripped his right wrist tight in an effort to stem the flow of blood, now steadily dripping onto the table. He could bleed to death while those two bastards sat there laughing at him. As for the girl, doe-eyed or not, she still didn't seem in Christian charitable mood. Lurking in her face was her

Indian grandfather's scalp-lifting trait.

Amos Bismark's voice hardened as he waved the gun under it's former owner's nose. Agent Blake knew also that it was a lie about Amos Bismark's family being of a peaceable nature. His eyes held all the venom his daughter's had.

'When yuh get back tuh Texas, tell the high and mighty Mr Slade tuh stop the hounding of mah friend, Mr Brown. And don't yuh come pussyfooting back or mah daughter might get real mad and plug yuh for real. *Adios*, Mr Pinkerton-man.'

Agent Blake got shakily to his feet still nursing his wounded hand. What would they say at head office? The scourge of the Indian Nations outsmarted by a girl. Those thoughts almost made him forget the pain of his wound.

Amos Bismark watched him leave then turned to Lazarus.

'The sooner we get the supplies loaded, Lazarus, and head back tuh the Hacienda the easier ah'll breathe. Slade's liable tuh have sent a company of Texas Rangers splashing across the Rio Grande tuh fetch yuh in.'

As Amos Bismark got up from the table he asked his daughter how she knew that the fat man was a Pinkerton agent.

'I didn't,' she replied. 'I saw him leave the

cantina just after you and Lazarus entered. He spoke to a man at the hotel then came back here. He seemed in too much of a hurry and looked as though he had a lot on his mind to have been a salesman, so I followed him in.'

'That's when ah stopped Lazarus from getting his fool head blown off,' said Amos.

'The expressions on both your faces,' said Elizabetta, 'told me that he was not just passing the time of day with you or trying to sell you something and then I noticed the gun.'

'Yuh say that there's another man...'

Elizabetta smiled. Lazarus still thought it was one of the sweetest things he had ever seen. 'It's been taken care of, Father. I sent Miguel and a vaquero to tell the man and any other friend of the fat man that they were not welcome in Bermejillo. Did I do right?'

Amos Bismark roared with laughter. 'If yuhr old grandpappy Santos was still alive he would've been mighty proud of yuh, daughter...'

Before he reached his hotel Agent Blake had regained a little of his former confidence. After all, he thought, one minor setback doesn't mean that the battle was lost and he began to think of a plan that could, even at this late stage, lead to a successful conclusion to the assignment. The sons-of-bitches had hurt more than his hand, the pride of the Pinkerton International Detective Agency was at stake.

Also what Amos Bismark and his blood-thirsty daughter did not know was that he had two men as a back-up team. The plan was quite simple. He would set up an ambuscade just outside town. Catch them on the hop as they drove the wagon-load of supplies back to the Hacienda. A plain old-fashioned drygulching. Agent Blake surmised that Amos Bismark would probably have at least three men with him. A grand total of six, for the girl had to be counted as good, if not better, than any male gunhand. Even so, three men throwing down on them from the shelter of a dry wash should easily overcome that opposition.

To be fair Agent Blake admitted to himself that bushwhacking was not quite up to what he felt should be the standard of pure detective work. But a hand had to be played as it came. A bow-legged Mexican standing at the door of the hotel interrupted Agent Blake's prospects regarding the optimistic outcome of his present case.

'Senor,' the vaquero said.

'Yes, what is it?' Agent Blake asked impatiently, eager to get his plan rolling. 'Those two hombres, friends of yours, have left, Senor. They told me to tell you that they have urgent business elsewhere.' The vaquero gave a lop-sided smile. Agent Blake's blood ran cold. He had never seen such a mirthless smile on such a frightening face. He put it down to the white-fleshed crooked scar that ran from the man's left ear, down and across and under his chin, that drew that side of his face into a permanent villainous sneer. God, he thought, a half-savage girl and a savage-face man. What manner of people live at the Hacienda Torrea-de-Carros?

Trying to hang on to what was left of his pride Agent Blake said,

'Oh, they have, have they? I'm much obliged to you, Senor, for letting me know. I'll be leaving myself as soon as I get my things together. I've no further business here also.'

The Mexican's smile broadened, pulling his face into an even more gargoyle-like expression. 'A wise decision, Senor,' he said.

As he climbed up the stairs to his room Agent Blake thought about Jason Slade and his Stonewall Jackson suggestion. It would take a blood-letter like General U.S Grant to wheedle out Mr Brown from the Hacienda Torrea-de-Carros.

Nineteen

Agent Blake cast a professional glance at the drinkers in the cantina and didn't like one little bit of what he observed. A real rogues' gallery. The evil, suspicious looks he was getting from them, the only gringo in the room, gave him the same chilling yet dry throat feeling that the wildcat daughter of Amos Bismark had.

'You must try again, Mr Blake,' Mr Robert T Jopling had told him when he had returned to the El Paso office and explained the situation regarding the non-taking of the negro, Mr Brown. 'I've passed the report of your failure to apprehend the black on to Mr Allan.'

Agent Blake inwardly winced. It was all very well and good Mr Jopling telling him that, but Mr Robert T bath-and-clean-shirt-every-day Jopling hadn't to do the dirty work. No siree. He was not up front. He'd been a desk man since he had joined the Agency. Never operated and lived with men who not only looked capable of cutting their own grandmothers' throats but more than likely had. Plus a few more of their close relatives also.

Mr R T Jopling continued; 'Mr Slade's a big man in these parts and it would be bad publicity for the Agency to fall down on this one. Hold back our future expansion. Mr Allan has telegraphed that we must spare no expense, the sky's the limit, his very words. As far as he's concerned,' Mr Robert T Jopling paused for dramatic effect, 'anything goes as long as we can get that negro out of Mexico.'

Me, not *we*, Agent Blake savagely thought. Aloud he said:

'It will be very difficult, Mr Jopling, as I said in my report the Hacienda Torrea-de-Carros is a hard place to get to. Surrounded by desert and watched over by bloodthirsty Apache. Without Mr Amos Bismark's say-so a man wouldn't get within shooting distance of the place. You'd need a regiment of U.S Cavalry and the Apache would definitely not allow them free passage. It would be a massacre.'

R.T smiled condescendingly at Agent Blake. 'M'be so, m'be so. But this time we'll try different tactics. We'll take the girl...'

Agent Blake's mouth dropped open. 'The girl,' he gasped in astonishment.

Robert T Jopling positively beamed. 'We use her as a bargaining counter. We have your daughter, Mr Amos Bismark, you have our

116

negro.' Then noticing the doubts on his agent's he added, 'Mr Allan Pinkerton himself came up with the plan.'

'It's...it's unethical,' stammered Agent Blake. 'Why, suppose some harm should befall the girl?' Not that he should fear on that score. In fact he pitied the man who tried to corral her but he wasn't going to let Mr High and Mighty Jopling know that. It was just that the plan ran counter to all his ideals of how a Pinkerton operative should work. 'We could be charged as accomplices to murder,' he finished off.

Mr Robert T Jopling remained silent.

'How do you propose to kidnap the girl?' R.T Jopling kept a still tongue. Agent Blake looked aghast at him. 'Surely not me!' his voice a high-pitched squeak of protest.

'Tut, tut,' chided Mr Jopling. 'Not kidnap, Mr Blake. That's too strong a word. We don't expect you to do the actual kid...er taking of the girl. The Agency has a contact in the village of Los Neves, in Durango, who has the ear of certain men whom he believes could successfully pull off this delicate operation. Your task will be to see to the financial arrangements and that the men picked are really up to the job. We don't want to throw good money away, do we...?'

Agent Blake was only half-listening to Mr R.T Jopling. He was trying to figure out just how far that other high and mighty so-and-so, Mr Allan Pinkerton, had put him out on a limb.

'...Our contact, a Senor Primitivo Agailar, will meet you at the Cantina de la Rosa a week from now. He will confirm, or otherwise say so, that the plan can proceed and arrange for you to talk to the man who will head the operation. You can make your point direct to him about the girl's safety being paramount or payment might be in jeopardy.'

Agent Blake shrank even further into his chair. How the hell does one tell a Mexican brigand and his men that their due has been unavoidably held up? And still keep a whole skin?

It was a disturbed Agent Blake that rode south once more. Robert T Jopling's final words still rang ominously in his ears. 'We are relying on you, Agent Blake. Mr Allan Pinkerton will be watching your progress with great interest.'

Agent Blake tried to ignore the glares he was getting. The Cantina de la Rosa, he sniffed in disgust; thieves' kitchen was a better name for the saloon. One thing he had found on his last brief trip below the border was that the fancier the name the bigger the dump. He had seen cleaner and better furnished bums' shacks in the Chicago stockyards. From a dark hovel of a room behind the two deal planks resting on barrel heads that passed for a bar counter he heard the braying of a burro.

The owner had put a bottle of some liquor or other and a greasy rim-nicked glass on his table and demanded payment. Agent Blake had paid up, not willing to annoy the owner any more than he had done by coming into the cantina. But he would rather sign the pledge than partake of the yellowish cloudy liquid in the bottle, brewed, he had no doubts, especially for gringo pigs. His contact, Senor Agailar, a small, shifty-eyed, oily-looking and talkative man, given to much arm waving and swearing of oaths on his sacred mother's grave, that must have had her corpse spinning round in its last resting-place, told him of his long friendship with the General and the General's reliability to carry out the taking of the negro, if the price was right. He had left him on his own after imparting the information that the General himself would soon be riding into Los Neves to see him and to discuss the finer points of his plan—the smile became oilier—and how the payment was to be made.

Earlier that week, Senor Agailar had stood outside General Sabas Urbina's cave in the bandit's hole-up, nervously twisting his hat in his hands, anxiously waiting for the General to finish his siesta. The General had an unstable temperament, Senor Agailar knew that he could be greeted like a long-lost brother or if the General had not slept off his last bottle of tequila or his latest woman had not satisfied him he could see the day's end buried up to the neck in the handiest ant-hill. And that was on a good day. Today was definitely a bad day. The General was having a run of ill-fortune. The dustclouds of his Tropa no longer guaranteed food and wine from the terrified peons, praying to the Holy Virgin that this time The Butcher, a title fearfully earned, would not violate their wives and daughters. How could the General have known, reasoned Senor Agailar, that the last young girl he had raped had only been a guest at the rancho and that her father was a *grande politico* in Mexico City? Big enough to send a full regiment of Federal cavalry, with two cannons, to avenge his daughter's deflowering.

The Federalists fought a real war. They had shelled the General out of his stronghold, the place of sweet water and many sweeter senoritas, and made him live like a rock lizard in these caves. So Senor Agailar could only stand and sweat and pray that the General's bed companion had special skills in the art of making love.

General Sabas Urbina pulled aside the blanket from the cave mouth and stepped out into the daylight. He eased his pants at the crotch, broke wind loudly, then squinting at the sun's glare, saw Senor Agailar. His face broke into a gold-glittering smile of welcome.

'Ah, *mi bueno amigo!*' he waved an arm in greeting. 'Come inside, my friend, drink a little tequila with me then we will talk about this business you have told Zalarzo about. Business that will bring me much dinero.'

'*Si, mi* General.' Senor Agailar's heartbeats returned to normal. He would sleep in his own bed tonight.

Inside the cave he caught a fleeting yet tantalizing glimpse of broad, sweeping buttocks and breasts as round and full as ripe melons as the girl pulled her shift over her head. Reluctantly he tore his gaze away. The General was so very touchy where his women were concerned. The General slapped the girl on her ample behind.

'*Fuera! Fuera! Muchacha.* Go, girl!' he shouted. 'I have business to talk with my good friend, Primitivo, here.'

121

The General's eyes widened in disbelief as Senor Agailar explained the instructions he had received from El Paso. He shook his head in wonderment.

'I always thought that the Yanqui gringos were loco. Now I know they are. Gold for a Criollo? A girl, I understand...but not for a black man. Are you sure that this is so?' He glared suspiciously at Agailar.

Senor Agailar could feel the ants biting again.

'I swear it is so, *mi* General, on my mother's grave, I swear!' he babbled the words out. 'There will be a gringo at the Cantina de la Rosa in two days time. He will confirm that all that I have told you is true.' He looked pleadingly at the General as he saw that the greeting smile had gone.

Could it be a trap set by the Federalists, the General asked himself. *Nada.* Not with gringos involved. The Federalists and their cannon had prevented him from collecting in his tributes from the villages, causing his men to grumble about the lack of women to pleasure and good wine to drink. With the gringo gold he could move further south and although it went against his taking nature, he could use it to buy the good things for his men until the Regulars got called back to their barracks in Mexico City and Durango was once more his again.

'I will see this gringo from El Paso,' he told Senor Agailar. 'If things are as you tell me and I get the gold, there will be payment for you also.' The General stood up. 'Tell the gringo that I will see him at noon on the day he arrives at Los Neves: *adios, amigo.*'

Agent Blake heard the sound of horses pulling up outside the cantina then dust billowed in through the beaded doorway curtain forming yet another layer of grit on the furnishings and bottles. A man came into the cantina quickly followed by another. The first man, a medium-built Mexican, looked in his direction then in a pigeon-toed walk came across to his table, spurs jangling loudly. The second man dogged his footsteps. The big spurred man wore a faded khaki uniform and a broken-peaked army cap. The jacket had several buttons missing and was greasy with old food-stains. The hard, cruel face hadn't seen a razor for several days nor his black straggling longhorn, scissors. Agent Blake sniffed. He smelt like a well-used horse blanket.

So this was General Sabas Urbina, the Butcher of Durango. The fancier the name... But he had to admit that what the General lacked in military dress he made up for in martial appearance. Twin bandoliers of rifle reloads

123

were slung across his chest. Two heavy-calibre Colt pistols pulled at the waistband of his baggy pants and his right hand held a silver-mounted Winchester repeater rifle. From his left hand dangled a quirt. The man with the General had the ploughshare face and expressionless eye of a full-blood. Yaqui, Agent Blake opined. The Conquistadors would have had many a bloody tussle with his ancestors. He was as heavily armed as his General. Between them they could start a small war.

The General slapped his quirt on the table-top and yelled, '*Vamos!* Pronto!' and the cantina's normal customers hurriedly downed their drinks and took to their heels. Only then did the General sit down, the chair creaking under the weight of his armaments. He laid the Winchester down on the table and picked up the bottle of tequila and yanked out the cork with his teeth and pushed the neck into his mouth, only pulling it out when half its contents had disappeared down his throat. He belched and wiped the back of his sleeve across his mouth, adding a new stain to his jacket. The General was ready for business.

'You are the gringo from El Paso, the one with the gold, no?' he growled.

Agent Blake's temper rose. He'd be damned if he was going to be talked down by a greasy, stable-smelling cut throat. He hard-eyed him back.

'Mr Blake, General,' he said testily.

The General's smile did little to soften the brutal face. 'Meester Blake, we will talk about this nigrou who is worth all this dinero. What is so special about this man, Meester Blake, is he made of gold?'

'It is an affair of honour, General. The black man has done a great wrong to a wealthy Texas ranchero.'

The General's eyes lit up in understanding. 'Ah, honour, we know of it in our country, Senor. I killed my brother in a matter of honour. I found him in bed with my woman.'

The General's body shook with laughter, rattling the bottle and the glass on the table, and Agent Blake saw the full-blood's knife-slash mouth twitch. That, he thought, is the nearest thing to a laugh that gravedigger face is going to show. Unless he gets more cheerful when carving someone up. He would have to tread lightly and smile often dealing with these two characters. He cursed Allan Pinkerton for thinking up such a scheme.

Greedy anticipation replaced the smile on the General's face.

'You have the gold with you now, Meester Blake?'

Face straight, Agent Blake said, 'Carry gold around in Durango? How long would I have it? Everyone in the State is not as honest a businessman as you are, General.'

The glass and the bottle rattled again as the General burst into laughter once more.

'I like you, Meester Blake. I think that we can do business together.'

Agent Blake continued: 'The gold will be paid in two parts. Half when the girl is taken ...' He raised a hand to stop the General's protest. 'Put yourself in the position of my clients, General. They do not know but what you would pocket the gold and head south, breaking their agreement. They know that you are having trouble with the Federalists.'

'But you have my word, Meester Blake,' the General said.

'So I have, General, so I have, but I'm only a small part in this operation. I have to do what they order me to do.' Agent Blake smiled across the table. 'I'm not a General. I will follow you north as far as Chihuahua City. You can send word to me there as soon as you have the girl. Two good men should do, then they can escort me and the gold to where you are hiding out. I want to do the negotiation with Mr Amos Bismark.'

'And the rest of the payment?' the General asked.

'When we hand over the negro to the U.S authorities at the Rio Grande.'

The bottle and glass shook for the third time as the General struck the table with his quirt in anger. He roared out his disapproval.

'*Madre Dios!* Do your gringo bosses think that I, General Sabas Urbina, am loco? It smells of a Federalist trap, Meester Blake.'

'I told you that the men back at El Paso are hard men to do business with,' Blake said. 'They will be worried in case you decide to hold on to the negro after receiving all the gold...try to sell him twice. But I can assure you, General, that they are men of their word. This is a private affair nothing to do with either the Mexican or American authorities. My neck's not going into the noose for the Federalists. So what can you lose by the arrangement, you have me and the negro? If things do not go to your liking you still hold all the aces.'

Agent Blake watched, tensed up to the last notch in his nerves, the different emotions crossing the General's face as his greed for the gold conflicted with the risks to his survival. Ignoring his fears, he had to show the General that he was the man in charge. Strength of purpose was the only thing the bloodthirsty bastard respected.

'One other condition, General; the girl must not be harmed in any way or the whole deal's off.' With a strength of purpose he definitely wasn't feeling he looked the Indian full in his snake eyes. 'You get my drift, gentlemen?'

'Do not worry about the girl, Meester Blake,' replied the General. 'She is of no matter. The gold will buy many such senoritas.'

'Good, then we have a deal,' said Agent Blake. He paused for a moment or two then he asked: 'How do you intend to get hold of the girl, General? It's wide open desert up there. Apache there also.'

The General smiled tolerantly. 'My *campadre* here is Zalarzo the Yaqui, Meester Blake. He could take a sleeping Apache maid's virtue in the middle of a tent full of Apache without waking any of them up.'

Zalarzo the Yaqui gave another steel-trap smile.

It could work at that, Agent Blake thought. A sneak attack by one man. The General wasn't just a pretty uniform. He got up from the table.

'I trust that you will make it safely to Chihuahua, General, and I'll expect to hear from you within the week. Good day, gentlemen.'

Agent Blake walked out into the street,

promising himself that when this assignment was over he would definitely finish with the detective business. Raise chickens, or hogs. Anything that would keep his blood pressure normal and prevent him, for fear, sweating his hide away.

General Sabas Urbina also had thoughts about Agent Blake's future, only more painful and permanent. Like how the little fat gringo would take being buried in an ant-hill or swinging over Zalarzo's slow fire.

Twenty

Through red-filmed eyes Zalarzo watched the girl, brown body glistening in the sunlight, come splash-stepping out of the water. Watched, with an involuntary hiss of pleasure, how the small firm breasts lifted as she raised her hands to clear the long dark hair from her face. Whatever arrangement his *jefe*, the General, had made with the fat gringo with the gold concerning the black hombre and the girl did not matter. The girl would be his woman.

This was the third time he had come to this place, stripped down to breech clout for easier passage, to observe the movements of the girl, his covering of the ground so silent that he had not disturbed basking lizards, making a fresh trail every time. This was the third time he had seen the lithe naked body of the girl as she bathed and swam. Only the thought of his *jefe's* anger at disobeying his orders and losing him the gringo gold kept him from taking the girl here and now.

He let the girl dry herself and put her clothes back on, only this time she would not ride back to the Hacienda. On the gringo's orders she was to be brought back to the *jefe's* camp unhurt and untouched. The Yaqui crept noiselessly out of the rocks to cut the girl off before she reached the flat. Suddenly he stopped and dropped back to the ground. His lips drew back in a vicious snarl. Apache. He drew his knife from his breech clout, nostrils distending at the prospect of some blood-letting. No Apache dog was going to take his woman. He crawled nearer, tense-limbed, ready for the final killing rush. Again the Yaqui stopped dead in his tracks. The girl was smiling and talking to the Apache.

Then what had been clicking away in his brain since he had first seen the girl became clear. The reason why the girl rode across Apache land unafraid and unescorted was that she was part-Apache. That discovery had the Yaqui drooling at the lips. An Apache virgin. His taking of her would be that much more pleasurable. When he was finished with her he would slash her breasts and slit her nostrils and send her back to her people. A gift from the Yaqui. She would be too ugly for any man to want to sleep with her. Never breed young warriors, white-eyed or Apache.

The Apache rode away and by the time the girl had mounted her pony he had gone from the Yaqui's sight. Elizabetta rode slowly back along the trail, reins loosely held, thinking of the black giant, the hombre **Lazarus**. Wondering how long he would stay at the Hacienda. A long time she hoped. The sudden noise of a rattlesnake beneath her mount's front legs made the horse snort with fear and rear wildly throwing her backwards from the saddle. Before Elizabetta hit the ground or even had time to give a cry of alarm, a brown shadow leapt from the rocks and grabbed her, striking her on the head with the handle of his knife. Elizabetta gave a little cry of pain before everything went dark.

The Yaqui slipped the knife back into his waist clout, tossed the dry gourds away and slipped the paper the gringo had given him, the paper that would bring them the gold, under the saddle of the girl's pony and slapped it on its flanks to hasten it back to the Hacienda. Effortless, he picked up the girl and slung her over his shoulder and in a looping trot headed back over the mountains.

News of the taking of Elizabetta and the price of her safe return reached Lazarus as he was shoring up the sandy banks of the stream at its double bend south of the Hacienda. The rider also told him that the Senor Bismark would like to see him at the rancho. The rage inside Lazarus flared up to white heat. He let out a loud shout of anger that sent the vaquero's mount skittering sideways in fright, almost unseating its rider. He picked up the long-handled hammer with both hands and with face working fiercely he brought it down and across his knee in one savage sweep, breaking the shaft in two as easily as another man might break kindling.

He would have to get back and get himself exchanged for Elizabetta and he swore that if she had been harmed in any way, somehow, even if he was shackled hand and foot going back to Texas, he would escape. Then what that Lord Almighty Slade suffered under the Apache moon-time would seem like a church get-together hayride. For the first time ever

Lazarus ill-treated a horse, savagely heeling it into a pounding, dust-raising gallop until the Hacienda was reached. Amos Bismark was waiting for him at the main gate. Lazarus could see no sign of any other mounted men, armed and ready to ride off and rescue Elizabetta. He pulled up alongside Amos and blurted out,

'You should have let me leave the ranch, Mr Bismark. Then this would never have happened.'

'Now, now, simmer down, Lazarus,' replied Amos Bismark. 'What's done is done, and besides it came mah business when that Pinkerton man threw down on me. No messenger boy of Slade's is going tuh stampede me into doing something ah don't want tuh do.'

'But it's me they want,' said Lazarus. 'So I'll get my gear together and if you'll tell me where they want me to show up for the exchange I'll ride out there pronto!'

Amos Bismark reached out and caught hold of Lazarus's mount's reins.

'Easy does it, boy. Don't talk such foolishness. Ah knew that yuh'd go off half-cocked, that's why ah came here tuh stop yuh. Elizabetta is in no danger yet. They'll give us a day tuh weigh up the chances of a rescue, they'll expect that. Then tomorrow we'll eat crow and hand yuh over. Or so they opine. If the Pinkerton man thinks that sidewinder of a General is going to hand over Elizabetta in exchange for yuh, all nice and gentlemanly like, then he's a bigger fool than ah took him fur. No sir, the General will want Slade's gold and gold from me for mah daughter. So yuh see if yuh went, ass-high, out there, yuh'd be wasting yuhr time.' Amos Bismark grinned. 'Then ah'd have to rescue yuh as well.'

'I'll get a squad of men mounted,' pleaded Lazarus. 'We can't just sit around doing damn all.'

'Too late, Lazarus,' said Mr Bismark. 'They're out there already. Just because ah ain't howlin' and scurrying about like a kicked cur dog it don't mean ah ain't got things movin'. No, not my heavy-footed vaqueros, Elizabetta's folks, the Apache, my ace-in-the-hole.' Amos Bismark pointed over Lazarus's shoulder. 'See that smoke on that far ridge? And the other tuh the left of the twin peaks? Apache scouts. Within hours the scouts will find where the General is holed up no matter how well hidden he thinks he is. Then there'll be more smoke pow-wow, pullin' in the whole blamed tribe. Come dark a coupla bucks will go in and get Elizabetta out. Shouldn't be too hard for people who've been stealin' horses off the Mex's for the past coupla hundred years or so.' The old rancher's voice stiffened: 'The Apache will attack once Elizabetta is out of the way and that two-bit General and the Pinkerton man will rue the day they ever saw the lands of the Hacienda Torrea-de-Carros.'

'I'd like to go with the Apache into the camp,' said Lazarus. 'Don't fret yourself, Mr Bismark, I can move sneaky-like if I have to. Indian Charlie taught me well. It was my doing that put her there and I'd like to think that it was my doing that freed her.'

Amos Bismark gave Lazarus a quizzical, lopsided look. 'Yuh're fond of her, ain't yuh? Ah'll see what ah can do. But it'll be up to the Apache chief tuh say who goes in.'

'Fair enough,' replied Lazarus. 'I'll stand by his say-so.'

Amos Bismark, Lazarus and Miguel left the Hacienda as the sun, dipping behind the sawtoothed ridges, killed the last of the light on the land, preventing any watcher seeing their going.

Twenty-One

Pinkerton-agent Blake was sitting on a camp stool in a much patched ex U.S Army Sibley tent. Opposite him, draped over a chair, as befitting his rank, was General Sabas Urbina. Zalzaro sat cross-legged on the floor to his left. The girl, Agent Blake having first-hand knowledge of the beast in the beauty, was bound hand and foot, and lay in the far corner of the Sibley. When the Yaqui had first brought her in, kicking and struggling, she had given him a look that boded ill for him if ever their positions were reversed. She had spat at the General and the Yaqui in what Agent Blake surmised as Apache language and by the expression on her face it was anything but wishing them well. Now she was lying silent and unmoving. Her Indian blood had allowed her to drop shutters over her eyes, making them dull and unseeing, cutting off her inner thoughts.

Outside he could hear the General's *muchachos*, his boys, some fifty of them, grandmother throat-slitters to a man, settling down for the night except for the strong line of pickets along the rim of the valley. From a military point of view Agent Blake had to admit that the General had chosen a strong position. Even if Amos Bismark raised enough men at the Hacienda to break into the valley the General assured him that there was a well-hidden back trail at the head of the valley that would provide an escape route if things got too hot. And besides, the General added, only a madman would attack the camp, day or night, when he did not know exactly where his daughter was. Any stray bullet from the attackers could kill or injure her.

In spite of the General's reassuring words Agent Blake's alarm bells were ringing. It had been over nine hours since the Yaqui had brought the girl into the camp and the watchers who had been keeping the exchange place under observation had returned just after dark reporting that no-one from the Hacienda had put in an appearance. The plan had been that the negro would be brought to the spot by Amos Bismark himself in daylight hours and if the look-outs were satisfied that it wasn't a trap one of the watchers would ride back to the camp. Then he would take out the girl for the swop. What disturbed Agent Blake's peace of mind was that the men had reported very little activity at all at the Hacienda, just the odd vaquero riding out towards the mountains. No Mr Bismark, no Mr Brown. No posses of armed men searching for Senorita Bismark's whereabouts. The plan was turning sour. He could feel it in his bones.

A quick exchange had been paramount to the success of the operation; to stop the General from getting impatient and thinking of how he could get gold for the three of them, the girl, the negro and himself. If the crooked bastard had not thought about it already. As a further lever in the note he had given to the Yaqui telling Mr Bismark the place for the exchange, he had let the rancher know that while he could guarantee personally the safety of his daughter in the short-term, any stonewalling or hesitation about handing the negro over could upset the other parties involved in the business and control of the situation could pass out of his hands.

Agent Blake looked across the box that served as a table at the General. He seemed asleep in his chair but every now and then the half-hooded piggy eyes would glint in the light from the lamp on the box-top. He had a good idea what the General was thinking. How much gold could he squeeze out of the deal. It did not need any skilled detective work to work out what the Yaqui's thoughts were. The pauses between the pulling at the bottle of tequila were becoming shorter and his looks at the girl getting longer and hotter. Agent Blake eased the pistol in its holster and prepared for trouble. It wasn't long in coming. The Yaqui struggled onto his feet and at first Agent Blake thought that he was going outside to relieve himself but instead he made his tangle-footed way to the girl. He knelt down at her side and grabbed the long hair and pulled her head back, his other hand riving at the drawstrings of her blouse. For a brief moment in time Agent Blake saw the shutters slip and caught a glimpse of fear in the girl's eyes. At least she is human, he thought, she can be frightened just like the rest of us. Before things got out of hand he leant forward and laid his gun hard against the Yaqui's head. The Indian slumped to the ground without even a groan and lay still.

Agent Blake brought the gun round and covered the General. The General's eyes were no longer hooded and sleepy. 'We made a deal,' he snarled angrily. 'The girl not to be touched or you'll not get the second payment of gold. Then what will your *muchachos* say? How far will one girl go amongst them?' Agent Blake's finger joint whitened as he took up the first pressure on the trigger. 'Now what's it going to be, General? Do you keep this,' Agent

Blake toed the Yaqui, 'This randy dog on a tight leash or is our deal off?' Then he said, the words almost making him puke, 'I thought I was dealing with an honourable man, a man whose word could be trusted.'

The General eyed the steady black hole of the pistol barrel, the steady hard face behind it. So the fat gringo had steel in him. The ants would soon eat that away. He smiled.

'It is only the tequila, Meester Blake. Do not worry, I will keep my side of the bargain. The senorita will not be molested.'

Agent Blake slowly lowered his gun, still keeping a watchful eye on the General. He was bathed in sweat and hoped that his fear had not shown in his eyes as the girl's had. The General's smile had as much sincerity in it as a python's facing a rabbit. He had walked a thin line ever since this fool deal had been set up. Risking his life with this band of cut-throats. He was well aware that just now he had stepped over that line. The General was not one to take kindly to a gun being pointed at him. He would have the ant-hill picked out for him already. That's if the Yaqui, when he came round, didn't have something a mite unpleasanter for him to take part in. He was only sorry that he had got the girl involved in this mess. Damn R.T Jopling and that went double for

Mr Pinkerton. Then he heard the girl say,

'For the kindness you have shown me, fat man, for not letting the Yaqui deflora me I will see that you die quickly, not roasted alive like the other two.'

The General, well used to threats from frightened girls, laughed out aloud. Agent Blake, thinking of his earlier alarm bells sounding off, didn't think that it was an idle threat at all. She was making a statement of fact. The little vixen knew that her father would be cooking up some scheme to rescue her and the confident look on her face before the shutters dropped again made Mr R.T Jopling's grandiose plan look mighty shaky indeed.

Twenty-Two

They were well inside the camp and Lazarus had not heard any complaint from Taza making too much noise. The first few yards had been pure hell as sharp-edged stones slashed at his belly and thighs, mixing blood with the sweat and bear-gease. But the thought of Elizabetta suffering the same fate as Luisa drove him on, ignoring the pain. Taza was still leading and

Lazarus was glad he was. He could not have found the Mexican camp even in a small valley like this without the aid of a compass.

It had been fully dark when Amos Bismark called a halt, the first since they had left the Hacienda. Lazarus couldn't see them but he sensed that they were all around him in the blackness, and the lifting of the hairs at the nape of his neck told him he wasn't mistaken. Several dark shapes closed in on Amos Bismark and Lazarus heard the old man's tongue clacking grunts and hisses. The rancher pulled his horse round and faced Lazarus.

'They're bedded down in a box draw about a coupla miles ahead, sentries strung out all along the rimline. There's a tent pitched up against the box wall that looks like the place where they're holding Elizabetta. Only one problem, it'll be tricky coming down into the draw on that side, loose rock, shale, straight up and down in parts. So whoever goes in is in for a spell of dirt-hugging right through the heart of the camp tuh get tuh the tent.'

'Belly-crawling won't hurt me none, Mr Bismark,' said Lazarus.

'Ah told the Apache why yuh want tuh go in, they can understand that. It fits in with their way of thinking. But the Apache yuh are going in with asks fur the right to knock yuh out or cut yuhr throat if yuhr presence endangers the attempt. That's also in their way of thinking. Does that strike yuh as fair, Mr Brown?'

Lazarus swallowed hard before answering. 'It does, Mr Bismark. I don't want to put any more lives at risk than I already have.'

Amos Bismark reached out and gripped Lazarus's shoulder hard.

'Move quietly, Lazarus, get her out safe. She's all ah've got,' his voice almost breaking.

'I'll kill every Mexican bandit from here to hell and back if I've got to, Mr Bismark, before I see her harmed,' Lazarus said grimly.

'Yuh and Taza, that's the Apache who's going with yuh, will go on foot from now on in. The main bunch will follow later. Even the Apache, a lot of them, can make the odd noise at night. We'll not attack until yuh come out with Elizabetta, unless we hear any ructions in the camp; then if yuh're still able tuh, keep yuhr heads low for there will be bloody murder done in that draw. It'll take a lot of blood tuh wipe out the insult of Chief Santos's granddaughter being held against her will. Off yuh go, and good huntin'.'

Lazarus shivered as the night air blew cold on his naked body. They were kneeling on the ridge and somewhere down in the black depths

of the draw was the bandit camp and Elizabetta. Four Apache warriors had escorted Taza
and Lazarus to the draw. He had stripped
down to his long drawers leaving his clothes
with Mr Bismark. On the rim he had watched
Taza remove his breech clout and naked as the
day he was born begin smothering himself with
grease. Lazarus knew that he couldn't afford
to fail his first test so reluctantly he pulled off
his drawers too and started plastering his body
with the throat-gagging grease. Taza signalled
that it was time for belly-crawling and Lazarus
wondered about the nocturnal habits of rattlers.
Did they sleep above ground? It was too late
to worry about that now, Taza had almost
vanished in the darkness.

They crept past the dark, huddled shapes of
sleeping men and the only lights Lazarus could
see were the odd reddish tips of the cigarillos
of men unable to sleep and the dim yellowish
glow of a storm-lantern through the canvas
walls of the tent.

A man, moaning and muttering in his sleep,
rolled over, his face almost brushing Lazarus's
hand. Lazarus halted and clenched a fist ready
for a killing blow but the restless sleeper's
breathing became deep and regular. Lazarus
moved on. Nearing the tent Lazarus tapped
Taza on the ankle. The Apache stopped and

waited for Lazarus to crawl up to him. By signs Lazarus indicated that he would go and scout round the tent while he, Taza, would stay on lookout. Taza nodded his head in understanding.

Lazarus saw the shadow of a man move across the light then vanish as the man dipped down out of range of the lamp's rays. He heard a voice raised in anger. Not clear enough for him to make out the words but he thought that it was the voice of the Pinkerton agent. Another voice, deeper, spoke back. That made three, at least.

Lazarus listened for several minutes but could hear no movement or talking. They could have settled down for the night. He began to shiver, the cold was killing him. It was now or never. He pulled out the knife that hung on a thong in the middle of his back and slipped it into the canvas and eased it slowly downwards. The heat returned to his body again as the tension and excitement set the blood hammering in his temples. He only hoped that the General wasn't cunning enough to have Elizabetta held in another place.

Agent Blake woke with a start. He must have dozed off. He took a quick look around the Sibley. Everything seemed as it should be. The General sleeping the sleep of the unjust. The

Yaqui still laid out. The girl lying bound tight. Then he noticed the shutters had gone from her eyes and the beginning of a smile was showing on her face. What had her Apache blood told her that he could not yet hear? Agent Blake heard a slight rasping sound on the tent wall behind the General. The lamplight glinted on several inches of steel cutting its way through the canvas. Two hands appeared at the rent, pulling it wide open, and into the tent stepped Mr Brown.

Lazarus took in the scene with one swift all-seeing glance, breathed a sigh of relief on seeing Elizabetta's smile. She seemed unharmed. The biggest threat was the man whose back was towards him. The General, by his uniform. He would have to take a chance with the Pinkerton man. Two strides took him to the back of the General's chair and in one swift deadly movement Lazarus brought his right arm round and under the General's chin and gripping the wrist with his left hand pulled and lifted.

Agent Blake, open-mouthed with fascinated horror, watched the black arm, as rigid as an iron bar, sweep across the General's throat. He saw the veins stand out on the negro's neck as he applied the pressure. Heard the sharp crack as the General's neck snapped. Dying before

146

the expression of what was happening to him was mirrored in his eyes.

Lazarus lowered the body back down into the chair. In a soft voice he called across to Elizabetta.

'The man on the floor?'

'Do not worry about him, Lazarus,' she answered.

Still breathing heavy Lazarus faced Agent Blake again.

'Do not reach for your gun, Pinkerton-man,' he panted. 'There's an Apache outside. He will kill you before you can get two shots off.'

Agent Blake sat unable to move. In less than ten seconds the grand plan of the best brain in the Pinkerton International Detective Agency had collapsed. He almost burst into tears. Lazarus ignored him and went to Elizabetta. As he came into the full lamplight Agent Bismark saw the blood and sweat-streaked torso and fierce, fixed, mirthless grimed face. He heard the girl giggle. Holy Moses, he breathed, Mr Brown was bare-assed naked.

Lazarus loosened the ropes that bound Eliza betta. When her hands were free she put her arms round his neck and kissed him full on the mouth.

'*Mi hombre,*' she sighed.

Agent Blake shook his head in disbelief.

Human nature never ceased to amaze him. Here was a man lying dead with his neck broken, a Yaqui Indian who could wake up at any moment howling for blood, and outside fifty or so equally murderously inclined plug-uglies, and a naked negro and a hellcat 'breed girl were billing and cooing like two turtle-doves.

Lazarus helped Elizabetta to her feet then prodded the man on the floor with his foot.

'What happened to him?' he asked.

Elizabetta's face darkened in anger. 'The Yaqui dog tried to have his pleasure with me. The fat gringo stopped him.' Savagely she added, 'Kill him.'

'He'll get that done to him soon enough,' replied Lazarus. 'Getting you safely out of here is all that matters. Now, Pinkerton-man, if you're still thinking of using your gun I'd better tell you how things stand. As I said, the Apache outside will kill you before you could pull the trigger twice. If he doesn't, the Warm Springs Apache will surely do. They don't take kindly to having their female relatives kidnapped. They're all around this camp waiting for us to come out. If things go wrong they'll come that bit faster. And may the Lord have mercy on your soul for they will have none. Then there's this Yaqui here, he won't be exactly full of brotherly love towards you when he wakes up.'

'What do you suggest I do, Mr Brown?' Agent Blake's voice was only a feeble squeak.

'You could come with us and take a chance that Mr Bismark will look kindly on you for saving his daughter from being raped,' said Lazarus. 'That's if he forgets that it was your doing that put her in that position in the first place.'

Agent Blake could not have put his options any clearer himself. He got up from the box.

'I'll take my chance with you and the girl, Mr Brown,' his voice back to normal.

Lazarus led the way through the opening in the tent, followed by Elizabetta and Agent Blake. Taza materialized at their sides as they stopped out into the open. Lazarus heard the Apache speak to Elizabetta after which she gave a soft laugh.

'Taza says,' she told Lazarus, 'that you move like an Apache. He calls you the Black Snake.'

With a little of the tension dying out of him and his blood count dropping to somewhere near normal Lazarus began to feel the chill of the night air again.

'I'll be a dying Black Snake if I don't get some clothes on soon. Let's get the hell out of here, keep together and move fast but quietly.

If we stir anything up make a run for it.'

Through slitted eyes the Yaqui watched them leave the tent. Any move to raise the alarm and he could start singing his death chant before ending up dead like his *jefe*. He could smell Apache, one, two, with the black man. But there would be many more waiting on the high ground for the signal to attack. The Yaqui had no special ties with the sleeping men outside, unaware of their likely fate.

His loyalty had been with his *jefe*, the General, and that died when the General died. There was no time to search through the General's belongings for the gold but there was still time to get back the girl before the Apache struck. He could cut them off before they started to climb the ridge and while their minds were occupied with making sure that they did not waken up the camp, he could grab the girl and disappear into the darkness. But not before he had slit the fat gringo's throat for making him lose face in front of his *jefe* and the girl.

The four crossed the flat swiftly and undetected. Before they started to climb out of the valley Taza paused and through cupped hands he gave a low mournful night-bird call. In an instant the call was answered once then twice from the high unseen rimline. The calls gave Elizabetta comfort and strength, made her forget her tight-held-back fears. She smiled in the darkness and reached out and squeezed Lazarus's hand.

'The Apache,' she breathed.

The Yaqui stopped trailing them. He had also heard. His face twisted in disappointment and hate. He had lost his *jefe*, the gold, now his woman. He had only his life left and he did not intend to lose that.

Agent Blake's heart was nigh on bursting as he scrambled up the bank close behind Lazarus. The negro was his only hope of hanging on to his scalp. The Apache were expecting three to come out, four if Mr Brown was there to put in a good word for him. If he wasn't then it would be too late to try and explain to the murdering butchers that he had just saved one of their women from being raped. Even if he could speak their heathenish tongue. They would have worked themselves up into a killing mood by now, not a talking one.

A voice away to his left shouted. *'Quien vive!* Who is it!' And stopped him worrying about his future and concentrated his thoughts on how he could stay alive right now. Hands snatched at him and he drew his gun and pistol-whipped his assailant. The man who had tried to hold him yowled in pain and dropped to the ground. Agent Blake swung his gun round and fired at the voices raised in alarm at his rear. He dropped to his knees as they returned his fusillade.

Lazarus was beginning to think that they had got clear when he heard the firing start up behind him. He cursed out loud. He did not know whether they had seen them all or that it was just Agent Blake that had drawn their fire. He could not take the chance. He wasn't going to lose Elizabetta at this stage in the game. Any wild shot could make a hit on any of them.

He shouted at Elizabetta, 'Go on! I'll try and delay them!'

'No, Lazarus!' cried Elizabetta, and tried to run back down to him. Taza held her and roughly cuffed her across the face and dragged her upwards.

He grunted in satisfaction to himself. The Black Snake thought like an Apache as well. If their positions had been reversed he would have stayed behind to protect the girl.

Lazarus sped down the slope. He could see by the flash and crack of a single pistol where Agent Blake was making a stand.

'Stop firing, Pinkerton-man!' he yelled and like a maddened buffalo crashed through the brush scattering the men who were shooting on the Pinkerton agent like chaff before the wind. Lazarus angled back up the slope well away from the spot Taza and Elizabetta were climbing, making as much noise as possible to draw the men after him. He heard the whining ping of slugs passing close by, then he was out of range.

The Yaqui, heading for his bolt-hole at the boxed end of the valley, heard the commotion on the slope and the thrashing of someone running fast through the brush and the pistol firing it was attracting. He stopped and quickly reasoned things out. It could not be the little fat gringo, not at that speed. It had to be the black man. He recalled the General's words about there being further gold when the black man was handed over to some other gringos at a crossing of the Rio Grande twenty miles north of the valley. But first he had to catch the negro. It would be a race against the Apache. The shooting had stirred up the whole camp, yet, cock-eared, the Yaqui could follow the black man's progress on the hillside above him. He set off running himself along the floor of the valley. When he reckoned that he had gained enough ground he cut up and onto the side of the valley. Elizabetta ran into her father's arms. 'Lazarus is still down there, Father!' she sobbed.

Amos Bismark put his arm round his daughter

and held her close.

'Don't worry, the Apache will find him.' He called over his shoulder. 'Miguel, take the senorita back to the Hacienda.'

Elizabetta drew away from him, eyes blazing. 'I'm staying until Lazarus is found!' she said angrily.

Her father hard-eyed her back. 'Yuh'll go with Miguel,' he told her grimly. 'What's about tuh happen down in that draw ain't fur yuhr eyes tuh see or yuhr ears tuh hear. Ah might have blood ties with the Apache but that don't mean ah have a powerful liken' tuh their methods of warfare. Now vamoose, girl.'

Lazarus eased up, satisfied that he had pulled the danger away from Elizabetta and Taza and that he had outrun his pursuers. He had no idea how Agent Blake was making out. He had given the Pinkerton man a chance but he chose to work with dangerous people and that brought dangerous risks.

The figure that sprang out of the darkness caught him completely off balance. A blow on the head sent him to his knees and into a deeper blackness. The Yaqui, panting with exertion, dragged the unconscious black man into a cleft on the hillside and slipped down alongside him. Taking the thongs from his boots he bound his prisoner hand and foot.

Twenty-Three

The new day was well on before Agent Blake crept, wild-eyed, dishevelled, pants bladder-stained-stiff, out of the brush. He had lain there since Mr Brown had shouted at him to stop firing. He had scraped frantically with one of his shoes a hole in the dirt for him to hide in. Could be his own grave was the depressing thought he had all the while he was digging. He lay in the shallow pit and raked the soil back over him, leaving his face clear to enable him to breathe, but also making him lose his glasses.

He heard the bird calls on all sides of him as the Apache came down into the valley. He felt something warm and wet spreading over his groin as they passed. Agent Blake shed tears of shame. The yells and screams below him as the Apache struck the camp gave his bladder no rest at all.

Daylight brought the real terror. The Apache were savouring their victory. The shrill woman-ish screams, dying away slowly, too slowly for Agent Blake's shattered nerves, to hoarse gurgles, of men being roasted alive over slow fires, rang frightening in his ears.

By high noon things seemed to have quietened down and the need for a drink of water was driving Agent Blake almost as mad as the screams of the tortured Mexicans had. He decided to risk it and left his grave, blinking in the sunlight as he peered cautiously into the valley. The blackened, shrivelled torsos still swung gently on the criss-crossed poles over the dead fires. But the Apache had departed. Agent Blake cried like a baby with relief. Slowly he scrambled unsteadily to his feet and quickly dropped prone again as his eyes caught a blurring movement below him. He rubbed at his eyes until they focused properly and saw the Yaqui, leading two horses, coming up the slope about a hundred yards ahead of him. The Yaqui stopped then bent down and seemed to be doing something with a rope. He stood up again and slapped one of the horses on the rump, causing it to walk forward. To his surprise Agent Blake saw Mr Brown, like his biblical namesake, rise slowly out of the ground. The Yaqui stopped the horse, picked up the negro and slung him over the second mount, fastening him on securely. Then getting onto his own horse, carried on up the slope leading the other by its reins.

Agent Blake was well aware that he owed the negro his life but could do damn all about trying to rescue him. He had lost his pistol and he did not think that rock-throwing at the Yaqui would help Mr Brown. He could go back to the Hacienda and let Mr Bismark know how things stood. M'be he'd round up some men and ride to the Lazy Y before Jason Slade carried out his promise. It was a long walk and he could bump into the Apache. At least he could try. It would ease his conscience.

Lazarus felt as though his body had been shot full of arrows. The Yaqui hadn't been gentle in getting him out of the cleft and his head still throbbed painfully from the blow that had knocked him out. Now trussed up, head down, like a Thanksgiving turkey, every step the horse took sent nerve ends twanging in agony. The Yaqui had not offered him a drink but to be fair to the Indian he had not touched water himself. If he had to wait for the Yaqui to get thirsty before he was allowed water he'd be long since dead.

By a painful twist of the head Lazarus saw by the lie of the sun that they were travelling north, to the Rio Grande and Texas and Slade's hanging tree. He was thankful that it wasn't going to be a slow fire-death and they hadn't hung him yet. The thought that he had got Elizabetta safely back to her father gave him a mite more comfort.

Twenty-Four

Mr R.T Jopling chewed impatiently at his lower lip. The only sign of life on the pack-mule trail across the Rio Grande was the man he had sent over to keep an eye on the trail idly pitching stones into the river. Where the hell was Special Agent Blake? It had been two days back that news had come to him that the girl had been taken. The deal should have been settled by now and the nigger once more on U.S territory well on the way to the Lazy Y and Mr Slade. He kicked bad-temperedly at the ground. That made him sweat even more and he was two clean shirts behind schedule. He had managed a bath every day. If standing knee-deep, bare-skinned, in tepid, murky, dead-dog-infested water, the butt of ribald comments from the foul-mouthed crew he had hired at El Paso, rated as a bath.

Further east lay the regular crossing with a

stage relay station and a ferry house where for a few cents a traveller could procure a hot tub-bath but this was a secretive operation. Kidnapping no less. A private law enforcment agency had no authority to pull a man out of a foreign country against his will. This was top brass law officer's work. And there was the local law to consider. Wouldn't do to rub them up the wrong way. The Pinkerton name might be able to open a few doors back east, even a bit of back slapping for services rendered as high up as the President's office, but in Texas they had no pull.

The law hereabouts was run by the Rangers and men with tin stars, Texas men. Men that didn't cotton on to fancy Northern law outfits coming in and running their show. Mr R.T Jopling gazed at the five men squatting round the fire, waiting for a smoke-blackened coffee-pot to come to the boil. Hard men even for west Texas.

There was another reason for being at this owl-hoot crossing. The main one. There was no more gold. That greaser bandit had been more than well paid already. The General would not bring his whole army to collect his due, that could stir up the Rurales. Four, five men Mr R.T Jopling calculated. The El Paso hardcases should be able to impress on the

General the foolishness of pressing his claim to the full. A shout of,

'Two riders coming in!' from the man on the Mexican side put an end to his ruminating.

'Get mounted,' he told the men at the fire then raising his voice he yelled across the river. 'Come on over.'

Mr R.T sat upright on his horse, his spyglass fixed on the two riders coming into view from out of the brush. He watched them until they reached the shallows then lowered the glass. Special Agent Blake was not one of them. The leading rider was an Indian of some sort. The second man was not riding at all. He was slung over his mount like a side of beef. Mr R.T Jopling smiled. It was the runaway nigger. Something peculiar about him though. He put the glass to his eye again. He quickly lowered it in astonishment.

'Holy Cow!' he gasped. The nigger was completely naked. 'You come with me, Mr Larson,' he said. 'The rest of you men stay by the fire, act naturally. We don't want to scare the Indian off.' Mr R.T gave a mirthless smile. 'He's expecting some gold, let's keep him thinking that way.'

The pair rode down to the water and as they splashed into the shallows the Pinkerton man gave Larson his instructions.

'You stay back a piece. Let the Indian see the bags on your saddle, he'll take them for the gold and stop him from being suspicious, let us get in real close. If he won't hand over the nigger peaceable or makes a sudden move, kill him dead.'

Zalarzo pulled up in midstream and waited for the two gringos to ride up to him. He had his rifle laid across his knees, ready cocked, for quick action. He had noticed the men at the fire but reasoned that if it was a trap he had time to pull the horses round and head back to the shore before they could get mounted. Once he had reached the brush he could easily pick them off as they crossed the river. He might be worrying too much. The ones to watch were the two coming to meet him. The Yaqui raised a hand to stop them coming any closer.

Mr Jopling and Mr Larson reined up. Out of the corner of his mouth Mr Jopling said.

'The red bastard smells something's wrong,' Mr Larson. Get ready to blast him from here.' He leant over and took the leather bags from Larson's saddle and raised them for the Indian to see. He gently urged his mount forward. Smiling, he said.

'I've got the gold, let's trade.'

Hawk-eyed, the Yaqui watched the tall

gringo ride closer, saw the smile and knew that he had ridden into a trap. He had seen his *jefe* smile like that just before he killed. He screamed out a death hullo and spurred his horse towards the smiling gringo, swinging up his rifle. He was too late. The .44 ball from Larson's Colt smashed into him high, tearing through his rib-case, covering the front of his shirt with blood, exiting under his right shoulder-blade in a ragged red mess of flesh and bone. The impact knocked him sideways off his horse, killing him before he hit the water.

Mr Jopling put out a hand and calmed the horse before grabbing for the reins.

'Let's go, Mr Larson. Ride ahead and get a blanket for this nigger.'

He could hardly wait until he got back to El Paso and wired the chief about the sucessful outcome of the operation. Then that nice long soak in a hot tub, and a clean shirt. Pity about Agent Blake. But that was the luck of the game. Lose some, win some.

Lazarus would as hell as like belly-crawl in front of Jason Slade. He stood as proud as cramped legs and aching back and still being clothed by a blanket would allow him on the porch of the Lazy Y ranch-house. His hands and feet had been untied but four armed ranch-hands flanked him.

At the Rio Grande the man in the store suit, Lazarus labelled him as a Pinkerton man, had given him water and let him sit on his horse but with his hands and feet tied. He had asked him about Agent Blake. Lazarus told him that the nicest thing that could have happened to the agent the last time he saw him was that he had been quickly and cleanly killed by a bullet. The store suit man just grunted non-committally and given the order to mount up and ride.

Jason Slade strode onto the porch and looked at Lazarus.

'Yuh'll be going tuh town tomorrow, nigra,' he said. 'Tuh stand trial for murder.'

Lazarus stared back at him. 'It weren't murder, Mr Slade. It was an eye for an eye, a tooth for a tooth. Like you used to subscribe to according to Mr Bismark.'

Slade's jaws clamped tight on his cigar and for a while he remained silent, just looking. Then he growled.

'Take him tuh the bunkhouse. Let him wash then feed him. And get him some gear. Big Jubal's should be about right. No rough stuff, understand? Ah don't want him tuh get any sympathy from any nigra-lover that might be in court by seeing him carried in.'

163

Twenty-Five

Captain Walsh sat at ease in his quarters smoking an after-dinner cheroot. He was reading the latest back-east newspaper. He felt a glow of pride. The bold type headlines read...'Young Captain Inflicts A Bloody Defeat On Red Savages In Early Morning Battle'. Following on came a blow-by-blow description of the battle at Sweet Water as pictured by writers half a continent away.

The Captain drew contentedly on his cheroot. They would be reading it in Washington. It could mean his receiving orders to come to the capital to advise the Army Staff on how to conduct an Indian campaign. If he did get a Washington posting he would let his hair grow long, plainsman style. Wear a fringed buckskin jacket, not forgetting the big Bowie in the fancy woven sheath at his right hip. That would make the young belles of the Washington military dances bouncers heave. A knock on his room door abruptly ended the Captain's thoughts on the future possibilities regarding the development of his military career.

'Enter,' he said curtly.

Acting Sergeant Jackson stepped smartly into the room and saluted.

'Beggin' the Captain's pardon, sir, but the Troop's just heard that Lazarus...Sergeant Brown I mean...'

'Ex-Sergeant Brown,' corrected the Captain.

'Yes sir, ex-Sergeant Brown. He's at the Lazy Y. One of the big house servants has told Corporal Hall that Lazarus has been captured and is now tied up in the crew's bunkhouse. Tomorrow Mr Slades gonna haul him up in front of a hanging judge.'

The Captain remained silent, digesting what his noncom had told him. He knew he'd had doubts about the wisdom of recruiting negroes into active combat regiments. But he liked to think that he was a fair and just man, keeping his inbuilt racial views at bay. The fight at Sweet Water was beginning to blunt the edge of his opinions. He knew now that men with pride in themselves and the regiment would fight like veterans regardless of their colour. The Comanche were proving that every day. Why darn it, he thought, he'd back his Troop against any Troop in Caster's 7th up there in the Dakota Black Hills.

Without Sergeant Brown and Indian Charlie the only press he would have possibly rated could have been a two-line obit...'Young Captain killed by hostiles in his first skirmish on the Texas plains...' He was man enough to admit to himself that the sergeant had watched over him even in the Fort, kept him from making too much of a fool of himself until he had found his feet so to speak. He had even left him a legacy. The best Troop in the regiment. The sergeant had the skill to get the best out of his men without the usual top sergeant's bullying, and had instilled regimental pride into them. Acting Sergeant Jackson was a living example of his methods. And another thing. Since the sergeant had deserted the men had not shown any resentment against their officer but had kept up their high standard of combat efficiency in respect for their former sergeant. Captain Walsh pushed back his chair and got to his feet, chin thrust out aggressively, George Armstrong Custer fashion.

'Like hell they will, Sergeant. No bunch of ex-rebels are going to hang a Union soldier and certainly not one of mine.' He puffed fiercely on his cheroot. 'It's a ticklish situation, Sergeant,' he continued. 'I could go officially to the Lazy Y, and ask them to release Brown for him to stand trial at the Fort here for desertion. But Slade has a lot of pull and he would soon have him in civilian law hands...Slade's law in this part of Texas...and before the cell door had slammed shut he'd be organizing a necktie party.'

'We could get him out, sir,' Sergeant Jackson grinned. 'Comanche style. Knock at the front door and come in at the back.'

'Create a diversion, eh?' replied the Captain. The cheroot glowed red for a few seconds. 'There's still a sizeable herd on the ranch, isn't there, Sergeant?'

'Yes, Cap'n, several hundred I reckon,' said a puzzled Sergeant Jackson.

Captain Walsh grinned at him. 'Now I calculate that nothing would distract a bunch of cow-hands more than an honest-to-goodness stampede, especially a night one.'

The Sergeant positively beamed. 'We could put a fire under that herd's tail that would create such a hullabaloo that would send them scattering north as far as the Red. We could take away the big house, no-one would notice.'

'You pick me six good men, Sergeant, full kit, within the hour. No more or we'll be falling over ourselves and besides we want to keep this private...Troop business. I'll see to it that we leave the Fort legally.'

Just before lights-out Captain Walsh stood in front of his men. In a voice loud enough for whoever was on duty in the regimental office he said.

'I've noted you six men on our last patrol. You're sloppy. You broke all the rules of night-march discipline. Even a stone deaf Comanche would have heard us.' The Captain slapped at his thighs with his gloves. 'I'll keep you out all night if needs be. I won't have the standard of the Troop lowered. Right, Sergeant, get them mounted and move them out.'

In the Regimental Office the Adjutant said to the Officer of the Day,

'We have another budding glory boy Custer here, Jim.'

Twenty-Six

After they had left the environments of the Fort, Captain Walsh led his men north, north to Lazy Y territory; now they were standing dismounted in a small timber-filled hollow. The Captain and Sergeant Jackson scrambled up to the rim and gazed down to the forward slope. They could hear and smell the herd but the tar-barrel blackness of a moonless Texas night prevented them from seeing the cattle. Further away to their right they saw pinpoints of light, the lamps of the main buildings of the Lazy Y. Captain Walsh explained his plan of campaign to his sergeant.

'You take one man, Sergeant Jackson. Your task, to rescue Brown. But don't take any chances,' he warned. 'If you are spotted high-tail it out of there. We don't want three hangings tomorrow. I'll see to it that the herd stampedes.'

Back with the rest of the men the sergeant picked Trooper Robson, a small but hard barrel of a man. Ideal for close-up rough-house fighting if the worst should happen. The captain detailed one man to stay with the horses then gave out his final orders.

'Corporal Hall and you two men will come with me. There's powder in my saddle-bag, Corporal, dish out four equal shares. Oh, leave your firearms here, and that applies to you, Sergeant, and Trooper Robson. We might all end up in front of a court martial so we don't want to take part in a gun battle and face murder charges as well. Also take off your jackets, brass buttons can be seen in the dark and could identify us. We want to leave Slade guessing just who was responsible for the rescue. Any questions?'

'Beggin' the Captains's pardon, sir,' Sergeant Jackson said. 'Don't you think that it would be advisable to put some of this black polish on your face? Ours kinda melt into the background?'

Captain Walsh heard the men laugh softly yet it did not seem to offend him.

'Er...good thinking, Sergeant, hand it over. Right then, off you go, I'll give you thirty minutes to get into position close enough to effect a rescue before I light the fires and we'll all rendezvous back here, with or without Brown. Good luck.'

Captain Walsh looked at his watch. Twenty minutes had passed since the rescue party had slipped over the rim. All seemed normal in the direction of the ranch buildings. No extra lights and, thank God, no shooting. He shivered. Was it the cold night air or apprehension? What had seemed after a good dinner, a cigar and the best part of a bottle of bourbon, a derring-do was suddenly turning a little sour. But the Rubicon had been crossed. Sergeant Jackson would be waiting for him to do his part. Right or wrong it had been his decision, his command. He straightened his shoulders.

'Right, men, let's move out, quietly does it though.'

Keeping low to the ground Captain Walsh ran towards the herd. Corporal Hall and the

170

two troopers were circling the herd to come up on it at the rear and far side. He had given them strict orders that they must wait until they saw his powder-trail lit before they lit theirs, and to make their individual ways back to the horses. It was every man for himself. He sensed rather than saw a movement closing in on him from his left and flung himself to the ground, hardly daring to breathe.

Above the snuffling and snorting of the restless cattle he heard the twanging tinny sound of a jew's harp. The rider passed his front almost within touching distance. The cow-hand sat easily in the saddle, back towards him, one leg draped over the saddle-horn.

Captain Walsh waited until the thrumming music faded away before he moved forward, on his hands and knees, taking no chances that his silhouette could be seen by a man on a horse. His right hand slid wrist deep into something soft. Something that smelt anything but sweet. The captain swore under his breath and again had doubts about suggesting such a harebrained scheme.

Undaunted by his thoughts the captain crawled within a few feet of several sleeping cattle, their steaming fug gagging at his throat. He laid a powder-trail from where he lay right up to the backsides of the nearest longhorn then

171

scrambled back to the beginning of the powder-line. He slowly counted to a hundred to give Corporal Hall and the troopers time to lay their fuses then he struck a shielded match and touched it off. The sizzling line of flame lit up the night sky and singed off his eyebrows. Over his shoulders as he sped back into the safety of the darkness he saw three more streaks of flame. He heard shouts of alarm as the frightened cattle, snorting and bellowing, got to their feet.

Sergeant Jackson peered cautiously round the corner of the bunkhouse. The only door into the crew's quarters was in the middle of the porch. By the light from the solitary lantern that swung from a porch beam he could see a man sitting on a chair keeled back against the bunkhouse wall. Across his lap the sergeant could see the glint of a rifle barrel. He licked his lips nervously; any minute now he thought. That's if Captain Walsh had managed to sneak down to the herd without being discovered. He had hardly time to worry about the thought when from across the blackness of the plain four orange streaks illuminated the herd followed by a sound like a thunder rattle. The herd had spooked. The sergeant grinned at Trooper Robson. Halfway to success.

The guard lept to his feet, upsetting his chair,

rifle clattering unheeded to the floor. He stood for a moment in disbelief then yelled into the bunkhouse.

'Stompede! Stompede! Grab yuhr pants!'

In no time at all men were erupting out of the doorway, shirt tails flapping, pants half pulled up, cursing and swearing at having their sleep disturbed, and heading for the horse corral. Lamps appeared in front of the big house and the sergeant could hear orders being shouted out by someone in authority. Slade, he hoped. If the rancher was in charge he'd have every hand on the spread out to stop the herd. No man would hang back when Slade was doing the calling.

The porch was cleared of men and Sergeant Jackson said, 'Keep close to the wall, out of the light from that lantern. It seems that all the crew are riding out to stop the herd but there m'be someone in the ranch-house and if they see two men at the bunkhouse they might come over to find out why we are not with the rest of the hands. Then we'll have a fight on our hands.'

The sergeant drew back sharply as a cowhand stumbled onto the porch, hopping on one leg as he struggled to put his boot on, swearing all the while he did so. With one final curse he stamped down his foot then ran across to the horse corral.

'My, my,' whispered Trooper Robson as he followed the sergeant along the porch. 'What purty language white folk use.'

Both men slipped unobserved into the room. By the flickering shafts of light from two low-wicked lanterns on the long eating-table they saw the huddled figure of Lazarus crouched in the far corner.

'Stay here,' said the sergeant. 'In case a cowhand remembers that he forgot to put on his pants. You know what to do but keep it quiet and don't make the injury permanent.'

Trooper Robson bared his teeth and lifted a ham of a fist.

'I'll just tap him, Sergeant.'

'Corporal Jackson, Trooper Robson? Is that you?' Lazarus called out.

'It sure is, Lazarus. But it's Sergeant Jackson now. I got your rank after you took off. Are you roped or chained?' he added as he went across to Lazarus.

'Roped, but what the hell are you doing here?'

'Why, we've come to rescue you,' explained Sergeant Jackson. 'Did you think the Troop was going to let Slade string you up.' He slashed at the ropes with his knife. 'Can you walk?'

'Yeah, I can walk, just a bit stiff that's all.

174

I suppose it was some of the Troop that started the stampede? There'll be hell to pay when Captain Walsh finds out about tonight's work. You'll be busted and all of you will end up in the stockade.'

'The Capt'n will be alongside us then. It was him who spooked the cattle. In fact the whole operation was his.'

Lazarus was too surprised to answer him.

From the doorway Trooper Robson growled, 'Are you two coming or are you going to spend the rest of the night jawing? The boys and the Capt'n will be biting lumps out of their saddles with worry.'

Twenty-Seven

Captain Walsh waited impatiently for the return of the rescue party. His three men had got back safely and were telling the horse guard all that had gone on. The ranch was quiet once more now that the herd was probably halfway to the Red by this time. He could still taste the dust of their wild passage.

'Here they come!' called Corporal Hall. He gave a little cheer. 'Three of 'em, sir.'

Captain Walsh strode over to the foot of the slope and met them.

'Well, ex-Sergeant Brown,' he said. 'This is a fine pickle you've got yourself into. You should've come to me when you found Indian Charlie. You of all people ought to know that the Army looks after its own. What are we going to do with you, eh?'

In the dark Captain Walsh felt the men crowding in on him. The tension was as electric as a plains summer storm.

'I owe you at least one favour, Brown,' he continued. 'I know you and Charlie looked out for me when we were on patrol and you'd get no justice in Texas, not from Slade and his breed, so I'm giving you a chance to ride away from it all. There's a horse and a canteen of water back there. Its owner is being chased by several hundred frightened longhorns.'

'Corporal Hall,' the Captain barked. 'You will hand Mr Brown your pistol and I trust that you can explain to the armourer, a friend of yours I believe, how you came to lose it.'

White teeth gleamed in the dark as the laughter broke the tension.

'There's a rifle in the saddle boot, get some extra shells from the men, so at least you've a fighting chance to make it to wherever you intend to go. But I must warn you, Brown, that if our paths cross again I'll take you in to stand trial for desertion. I'm not blacking my face and crawling knee-deep in cow-shit again.'

'That's more than fair, sir,' replied Lazarus. He stood to attention and gave the Captain a parade ground salute. 'Good luck in your command. You've got the best Troop in the regiment, if you kick their butts now and again.'

More laughter rang round the hollow.

'And good luck to you, Lazarus.' Captain Walsh stretched out a hand. Lazarus gripped it in a firm handshake.

Captain Walsh rode at the head of his men. The faint glow of the coming dawn was rapidly bringing the colours back into the plain. He breathed in deeply, favouring the cool sweet early morning air. Behind him he heard Corporal Hall's deep bass voice break into song. Soon the rest of the section joined in. It was the first time his men had sung in his presence. Previously some of them had not even spoken to him unless replying to a direct command. He had been accepted at last and the grand feeling that gave him moistened his eyes.

Proudly the Captain straightened his back. To hell with the tight-panted, white-gloved tin soldiers in Washington D.C. This was what soldiering was all about. Why dammit, he *would* buy himself that fancy buckskin jacket and let his hair grow long, glory boy George Armstrong Custer style. He threw back his head and sang in unison with his men.

'Buffalo gal ain't you comin' out tonight, comin' out tonight...'

The same dawn greeted a red-eyed, gut-churning mad Slade. He stood on the porch of the big house watching equally red-eyed weary men herding small bunches of cattle back to the ranch. His cigar was only a soggy bitter-tasting mess in his mouth. He spat it out and called across to Ketch.

'Leave what's left of the herd out there. They'll settle down at the first water. Get the men bedded down 'til noon then I want them saddled up and loaded for war, rations for at least a week.'

'Who do we reckon to be fighting, boss?' asked Ketch.

Only one person could have pulled an Indian trick like this to get the big nigra away, that sonuvabitch, Amos Bismark. The nigra soldiers wouldn't have the brains to pull such a stunt and he couldn't see any white officer putting his career on the line for a nigra. No, it had to be Amos Bismark.

'Why, Amos Bismark, who else. Ah intend to burn the Hacienda Torrea-de-Carros about his ears and settle this nigra business once and for all. Should'a done it my way before now instead of wasting time and money with bounty-hunters and fancy-smelling Pinkertons.'

Twenty-Eight

Lazarus rode south, for the border and one last look at the sweet-smiling Elizabetta before moving further south. His presence at the Hacienda would only bring trouble. Next time they might not be so lucky and he had a gut feeling that trouble, big trouble, was not that far behind him. Lazarus guessed Slade's reading of the stampede and his rescue, that Amos Bismark had been the man behind it all, and the Texas rancher would want his ex-pardner's blood to wipe out the insult.

He would tell Amos Bismark about Slade's possible reasoning concerning his escape and if they wanted an extra gun at the Hacienda until Slade's next move became clearer he'd stay. After the threat had blown over he would move on.

The dog-leg trail dropped down from the high ground, and cutting across a wash, stretched over the flat to the bottom lands of the Rio Grande. Lazarus had travelled a lot slower than he had hoped but he had seen smoke talk on the high rims all morning. Just south of the wash, on the black-faced bluffs on the far side of the valley. Lazarus at last saw the reason for the smoke signals.

The war band was set in a long straggling line against the sun as they picked their way down one of the lower razorbacks, their mounts' haunches brushing the ground with the steepness of the grade. They could be Warm Spring Apache, Elizabetta's kinfolk, Lazarus reckoned; but he had no great hankering to ride closer for a look-see. More likely they were Comanche, heading for their stronghold in the Sacramentos. If the hostiles were still on the prod he couldn't see them getting their horses in a sweat for one lonely scalp. The ridge the war band was descending met the valley floor north of the wash. If they crossed the gully then there was a good chance that he had been wrong and the red devils did want his hair.

He waited, backaways from the trail, as the war band reached the valley floor and came south and dropped down into the wash. If they did look like coming in his direction before he showed them his dust he would cut loose with the Winchester, lay two or three of the band low just to let the rest know what sort of opposition they were up against. The war band stayed in the wash and Lazarus's conclusion was, being a stream in there, that the hostiles had stopped to water their ponies. He tongue-clicked his horse into a walk and he kept looking over his shoulder at his back trail in case of a sneak attack by one or two of the bucks until he was well clear of the wash.

Three miles further south Lazarus heard the sound of gunfire. The war band had been after bigger game than him. It could be Slade and his men, even a Texas Ranger patrol or a scout detail from the Ninth, his own Troop, even. And that thought made Lazarus pull his mount's head round and ride north.

Irregular bursts of gunfire echoed in the valley and where the trail dipped into the wash powder-smoke hung in the air in yellow, blotchy clouds. On the far side Lazarus saw dark, still bundles that were men and horses, facing north, cut down as they had tried to escape from the ambush. At least they weren't Army, Lazarus noticed. The Buffalo Soldiers would have had a scout up front making sure that the trail ahead was clear. Only a man like Jason Slade, used to folk stepping aside for him and in a big hurry to even up the score, would ride bull-headed into an Indian trap.

The gunfire rose into a ceaseless roar as four riders, horses raising the dust, came up out the wash. Two of them fell off their mounts before they had cleared the edge. The remaining pair, lashing frantically at their horses, thundered towards the big rocks at the foot of the eastern bluffs. Half a dozen Indians burst onto the flat and took up the chase. A third rider slumped in his saddle and unable to hang on slipped to the ground. The Indians split up, three riding to the man lying in the dirt, three arrowing onto the surviving escapee.

Lazarus recognized Slade's horse but he did not hesitate in his actions. Even Slade did not deserve the fate the Indians would dole out to him if they caught him alive. He came storming out of the fold in the ground, sun at his back, reins between his teeth, throwing shells at the three pursuing bucks as fast as he could lever them into the chamber of the Winchester. Lazarus's sudden appearance threw the Indians into disarray, halting their chase. Time for him to get within accurate rifle fire range.

Lazarus pulled up his horse sharply and took an aimed shot at the only one of the hostiles that had a rifle. He heard the Indian's thin wail as he dropped over his pony's head. Two more rapid shots felled the other two before they had the chance to string arrows to their bows. Out of the corner of his eye he saw the bucks stop their grisly work on the body lying on the ground, jump on their mounts and come hell-bent in his direction. Lazarus hurrahed his horse into a gallop, clinging to its side Indian-style, punching off Dragoon loads across his saddle-horn.

A lucky shot brought one of the bucks' horses down in a tangle of legs and squeals; the remaining pair closed in on him, lance arms outstretched. The Dragoon's hammer clicked on a spent case and the war-painted hate-contorted faces whooped their triumph. Faintly Lazarus heard the double whipcrack of a rifle and two riderless horses skeetered past him. Slade lay behind his horse thumbing new loads into his rifle as Lazarus drew up beside him. Lazarus reached out a hand.

'Jump up behind me, Mr Slade!' he yelled. 'We've got a fighting chance, if we can get our backs up against those bluffs.'

Slade ignored him, carrying on reloading his rifle.

'Grab the hand, man!' pleaded Lazarus. 'I ain't about to lose my hair, so forget your blasted pride and let's get to hell out of it or you'll surely lose yours!'

'Ah think that ah've busted mah ankle,'

growled Slade, 'when mah blasted horse stepped into a prairie-dog hole, so ah'll only hold yuh back. Ride on, boy, while thar's still time. Ah've caused enough men's deaths today without wanting tuh add tuh the tally.'

Lazarus leapt from his horse and in spite of the rancher's bulk and loud protests lifted him up as easily as other men might pick up a child and laid him across his horse's rump. Quickly remounting he made for the foot of the bluffs. Behind him more hostiles were showing themselves along the wash rim.

They were sheltering behind a big rock that gave them a clear field of fire. Lazarus had led his horse into a gash in the face of the bluff and had joined Slade with all the fresh shells that he had for the Dragoon and the Winchester, and the water canteen.

'I'm low on reloads,' he told the rancher. 'M'be stop one frontal attack by the whole bunch if we hold them back from the rocks. If not...' Lazarus shrugged his shoulders.

Slade looked at Lazarus and smiled bitterly to himself. He'd been trying his damnedest for months to see the black man hang, now his stubborn pride was going to see them die together. And they had even just saved each other's necks already. His stupid pride had killed his wife and son. Amos Bismark had ridden over and told him that a Kiowa war band was out but he had put the protecting of his herd before the safety of his family.

The killing of his family almost broke him. Made him realize that all these years he had been living a lie. Putting the building of the herd above everything. Friendship, even. God forgive him, his only kin. Yet his stubbornness somehow wouldn't let him fully accept that fact. Made him blame his best friend, Amos Bismark, for his grief, and live out the lie. Now his mule-headedness had got his crew massacred. Men who had started cow-herding for him as boys lay butchered in the wash. At least he would try and make some amends before it was too late.

'Thar's still time fur yuh tuh make a break fur it, Mr Brown,' said Slade. 'Ah can hold them Comanche a while, give yuh time tuh get along the trail a piece.'

'I'll stay, Mr Slade,' replied Lazarus. 'One man wouldn't have a cat in hell's chance of stopping them if they came in one rush. Two just might wear them down, make them satisfied with what they've already took.'

'Don't be a stubborn fool,' Slade said angrily. 'Thar's no need for yuh tuh get yuhself kilt on mah account, Mr Brown. Ah've caused yuh enough trouble as it is. It comes hard fur a man tuh admit that he's been a stubborn-headed mule for most of his life and there sure ain't time, here and now, tuh apologize for thirty years of wrongdoing, but at least ah can get yuh off mah conscience. Just leave me yuhr rifle and git.'

Lazarus shook his head. 'We'll see it through together, Mr Slade, or I'll take you with me.'

Slade snorted in derision. 'A horse double-ridden wouldn't get a coupla miles over these bluffs before the red varmints caught up with it.' The rancher pointed his pistol at Lazarus. 'Now git on yuhr horse and ride on out and let an old fool live out his life the way he wants tuh or so help me ah'll save the Comanche the trouble and by the way things are shaping up down thar the time fur arguing about our situation is about ended; see, thar's another bunch of them coming along the trail.'

Lazarus looked at the dust-trail moving fast from the south. He studied it for several moments then grinned.

'They ain't Indians, Mr Slade. Never see hostiles ride in double file.'

Taking a longer look at the approaching column the rancher said,

'Tain't blue-bellies either; no shiny brass buttons or guidons flapping; too many riders for a Ranger patrol.' His face broke into a smile. 'Ah do believe it's that old hellbinder Amos Bismark and his Mex crew. But what in tarnation is he doing this side of the Rio Grande?'

It was Lazarus's turn to smile. 'Why, to save me from a Texas neck-tie party, Mr Slade.'

Amos Bismark, at the head of twenty armed-to-the-teeth vaqueros, glanced at his daughter riding alongside him. He used to lie awake at night worrying about how a girl just out of her teens could manage to run a big ranch and boss it over a half-wild crew. Not any more. It seemed that he was only just getting to know his daughter. It had been Elizabetta who had found Pinkerton Agent Blake, fancy store shoes slashed to ribbons, and feet dripping blood, more dead than alive, and had brought him back to the Hacienda. And hearing the news of Lazarus's whereabouts, raised the Tropa and sent word for him, working on the south range, to come urgently to the big house.

'We are riding to Texas, the Lazy Y ranch, pronto, Father,' she told him when he asked the reason for the mounted and armed men. 'Lazarus is being held there by an old friend of yours, Mr Slade. The little fat Pinkerton man was on his way to the Hacienda to tell us how he saw the Yaqui take Lazarus north. I found the gringo lost in the mountains. He is being taken care of and wishes us well as Lazarus had saved his life.'

Amos was all set to tell her that the small war she was embarking on was man's business but the steel-hard unblinking Apache look she gave told him that he was wasting his breath. He hoped that they were not too late and Lazarus hadn't already been hanged. The mood his daughter was in that news would turn her into a full-blood, liable to burn Fort Dodds to the ground along with the big house of the Lazy Y.

Miguel, riding point, rode back to the column. Amos Bismark raised his hand and the riders halted in a swirling dust-storm.

'A gunfight three miles up ahead, Mr Bismark!' he shouted. 'Comanche and two gringos holed up in the rocks. There's another trail away to the east that'll take us well clear of the trouble.'

Before Amos Bismark could issue fresh orders to his men Elizabetta cried,

'No, Father, we ride this trail!' her eyes wide with alarm and anxiety.

Amos did not question his daughter on how she knew it was Lazarus the Comanche had tree'd. The Apache had ghost dancers, spirit talkers, medicine men and suchlike who could see things written in the wind that the white

188

eyes couldn't see plumb in front of their noses. Curtly he rapped out,

'We ride this way, Miguel, but fast.'

Lazarus and Slade watched the oncoming riders peel off from the trail and sweep round in a tight half-circle, firing as they closed on the Comanche. The hostiles melted back into the wash and in twos and threes scattered for the safety of the high rocks. Two riders came across the flat towards them and Lazarus saw the slim figure and the long black hair tossing wild in the wind, Apache fashion. So she did care enough about him to risk her own life and had been strong enough to convince her father that it was her right to do so. He grinned broadly as Elizabetta rode nearer.

Amos Bismark nodded a greeting to Lazarus. 'Pinkerton Agent Blake told us yuh was took by the Yaqui. He came over the Candelarias on his hands and knees. Got a lotta grit, that dude.' He then looked hesitantly at Jason Slade. 'Ah didn't expect tuh see yuh, Jason, not hereabouts leastways.'

'Ah gathered that, Amos,' Slade grinned. It sure is a small world, ain't it? Ah take it that fine-lookin' gal is yuhr daughter, Elizabetta, that's her name, ain't it? She was only a babe-in-arms the last time ah saw her.'

'She sure was, Jason. That was twenty years

or so ago. A lifetime.'

'Too damn long, Amos. Too damn long fur a man tuh have been an ornery critter. Mah hard-headed days are over. Ah have no quarrel with Mr Brown now. When ah get back tuh the ranch ah'll put the word out that this is so.' Slade grinned wryly. 'If yuh can oblige me with a horse ah'll be on mah way. Thar's a lot of thinkin' tuh be done when ah get back tuh the ranch.'

Slade seemed to have physically shrunk. The blustering blow-hard shell had vanished, leaving an old old man beaten down by events he could not handle.

Amos Bismark turned to Lazarus. 'What's yuhr intention, Lazarus, now that Jason has called off the hunt? Give yuhrself up to the Army, do yuhr time in the stockade and re-enlist? Or ride south with us?'

Lazarus was conscious of Elizabetta watching for his decision showing in his face before he spoke. He smiled at her.

'I'll ride with you, Mr Bismark,' he said.

Elizabetta sweet-smiled him back. 'You can take that horse in the gully, Mr Slade,' she said. Then her smile became even sweeter as she looked at her father. '*Mi hombre* can ride up here with me.'

Amos Bismark pushed back his hat and

scratched his head.

'Well ah'll be durned,' he gasped. 'Her man! Why she's more Apache than her ma was. Yuh'll be getting an invite to a hitching soon, Jason.'

'Wait 'til mah foot mends up first, Amos, so that ah can have a dance with the bride.'

Amos Bismark winked at Slade. 'Don't just stand there grinning like a cat that's been at the cream, hombre,' he barked. 'Get up alongside her, pronto! Yuh know how tetchy she can get if folks don't do what she says.'

At a run the 'hombre' leaped up behind Elizabetta. His future wife heeled her horse hard and the pair of them, whooping and yelling like full-blood Apache, raced across the flat to the waiting vaqueros.

'Yuh're a lucky man, Amos,' said Slade.

Smiling benignly Amos replied. 'Ah sure am, *campadre*. Now ah'll see about getting yuhr crew decently buried then a coupla of mah boys will escort yuh back tuh the Lazy Y, then ah'll tell those two love-birds tuh hang fire on the wedding until yuh're fit enough tuh partake in the festivities.'

Jason Slade put out his hand. 'Ah, 'd like tuh shake on that, *campadre*.'

W